TOP
DOWN

TOP
DOWN

*A Novel of
the Kennedy
Assassination*

Jim Lehrer

RANDOM HOUSE

NEW YORK

Copyright © 2013 by Jim Lehrer

Published in the United States by Random House, an imprint of The Random House Publishing Group, a division of Random House LLC, New York, a Penguin Random House Company.

RANDOM HOUSE and the HOUSE colophon are registered trademarks of Random House LLC.

LIBRARY OF CONGRESS CATALOGING-IN-PUBLICATION DATA
Lehrer, James.
Top down: a novel of the Kennedy assassination / Jim Lehrer.
pages cm
ISBN 978-1-4000-6916-3
eBook ISBN 978-0-679-60350-4
1. Journalists—United States—Fiction. 2. United States.
Secret Service—Officials and employees—Fiction.
3. Kennedy, John F. (John Fitzgerald), 1917–1963—
Assassination—Fiction. 4. Political fiction
gsafd I. Title.
PS3562.E4419T67 2013   813'.54—dc23   2013007984

Printed in the United States of America on acid-free paper

www.atrandom.com

9 8 7 6 5 4 3 2 1

First Edition

Title-page image copyright © iStockphoto.com

Book design by Victoria Wong

*To the men and women
of the U.S. Secret Service*

TOP
DOWN

1

"Where Were *You?*" There it was—the most universal of questions we ask one another following an epic public event.

Now it was the title for a fifth-anniversary discussion at the National Press Club in downtown Washington. On that November 1968 noon hour, the complete question for the discussion was, of course, "Where were you on November 22, 1963, when John F. Kennedy was assassinated?"

I was delighted—excited, frankly—to be one of the three panelists invited to speak. And proud to be a club member because this was truly the center of my universe. The bureau offices of my newspaper, *The Dallas Tribune,* were on the fifth floor of the press club building on 14th Street, two blocks from the White House.

I had told my own story before. It seemed that everyone in America had at least ten times over. But this was the first time I did so in such a public way. More than three hundred people—most of them fellow journalists—filled the room.

The two other panelists spoke before me. The first speaker

was a wire service man who had been on the Washington news desk that November day. He talked about the emotional exhaustion of the conflicting pulls of duty and grief that gripped everyone taking in, writing, confirming, packaging stories from and throughout the world.

The second, a Washington-based network television correspondent who had been in the Dallas motorcade press bus, recalled the scraps of his and others' frantic searches for what had actually happened. Was Kennedy really hit? If so, where? Was he dead? Where did the shots come from? Had anybody been arrested? What was Jackie doing crawling back on the trunk of the limo after the shots were fired? Where could I find an eyewitness? Where could I find a telephone?

Perhaps I should have felt intimidated as the youngest and least experienced journalist of the three. But I felt that I matched the other two speakers for interest and delivery. My dad, also a newspaperman, always said I had "a gift of gab," a trait my mother saw as a good thing that could someday lead me from print to television. ("Mark my words, Jack," she said more than once, "you could be another Chet Huntley.") But I had absolutely no interest in ever being on television. I was a print man. I was a writer.

But I did spend more time than usual on exactly what to wear to the press club event. *Brainy newspaperman* was the look I was going for with my brown-and-black wool sport coat, gray slacks, and button-down blue oxford cloth shirt with solid dark brown tie. Back in Dallas I always wore a tie, but it was more often than not loose from the collar. That kind of style was okay for a local newsroom but not for a Washington correspondent. I did it up tight with a smart military half Windsor.

The other press club panelists spoke mostly from notes, while I had written out my story, which I read almost word for word after practicing several times in front of the bathroom mirror at my apartment.

When it was my turn at the podium, I began: "I was working as a reporter for an afternoon newspaper, *The Dallas Tribune,* on November twenty-second, 1963. My assignment was to cover the arrival of President and Mrs. Kennedy at Love Field, stay at the airport until they came back after a motorcade through downtown and a noon luncheon at the Dallas Trade Mart, and then report on their departure . . ."

In detail I told how I, at the behest of a rewrite man downtown just before the Kennedys arrived on Air Force One, had asked a Secret Service agent about the bubble top on the presidential limo. Was it going to be up or down when the motorcade went through downtown Dallas? It was strictly a weather issue and the early-morning rain had ended. The agent, Van Walters, after having some other agents check the situation, ordered the bubble top off the car. The early-morning rain had ended. I was there when Agent Walters gave the order. There was some loose speculation afterward among law enforcement people and others, which I reported, that the bubble top, if it had been there, might have prevented the assassination—or at least the death—of Kennedy.

I returned to my seat at the discussion table to what I felt was a dramatic silence. From my perspective, the audience had pretty much hung on my every word. It may sound like a lot of bravado, but I swear I even saw some wetness in a few eyes. Clearly, the agent's what-if suffering for having made the bubble top decision touched the audience.

A young man from the fourth row shouted out:

"What happened to that Secret Service agent—the one who ordered the bubble top off?"

"I don't know," I answered. "I lost track of him."

And that was how it all began.

"I DON'T KNOW. *I lost track of him."*

My words were quoted in the small Associated Press account of the event that went out to newspapers everywhere, including my very own *Dallas Tribune*. I hadn't expected any press coverage, but I was delighted by the piece. The *Tribune* had promoted me to its Washington bureau in late 1964 and, as the low man on the totem pole, it would definitely help to make a little here-I-am noise with the hometown editors.

It was just after eight o'clock Saturday morning—four days after the press club panel. I was in the bureau office putting the final touches on a Sunday story about the coming of new post offices in seven "fast-growing" Texas towns and cities. Under the leadership of Lyndon Johnson, the federal government was seen—and duly reported by the *Tribune*—as very much a growth industry in Texas.

"Are you the Jack Gilmore who spoke about the bubble top—the one quoted in *The Philadelphia Inquirer* yesterday?"

It was a woman—a young woman under some stress, it seemed by the sound of her voice—on the phone.

I confirmed that I was.

"Mr. Gilmore, I'm Marti Walters, and that Secret Service agent who you wrote about, Van Walters . . . well that was—is—my father," she said. "I must speak with you—in person, as soon as possible."

There was an undeniable urgency in her voice. When I was slow to respond she said, "We're talking life or death here, Mr. Gilmore. My father's life is at stake."

How could I pass up a summons like that? The Kennedy assassination had been the most important story of my journalistic life at that point and probably always would be. I had spent months on the *Tribune* team covering the post-assassination investigation and the unending aftermath developments, including the Jack Ruby trial. I had become the *Tribune*'s go-to reporter on the assassination, and even now from my desk in Washington I still considered myself such five years later.

Without hesitating, I agreed to Marti Walters's suggestion that we meet for Sunday brunch the next morning at a restaurant in the Washington Union Station.

"I'll be coming down on the train from Philadelphia," she said. "I'm short and skinny."

Trying to be funny, I replied, "No problem. You'll know me because I'll be the handsome one with the marine crew cut."

But funny was obviously not Marti Walters's thing as I was

met with silence. "I'll be wearing a brown-and-black-checked sport coat," I said, soberly.

"I'll find you," said Marti Walters.

SECRET SERVICE AGENT TALKS OF DEATH IN DALLAS!

To my knowledge, in the five years since the assassination no Secret Service agents had said much of anything to any reporters about what happened that day in Dallas.

Visions of headlines and glories danced in my head.

I SAW RIGHT away that Marti Walters was just a kid. She couldn't have been a day over twenty years old—if that. Clearly a college girl. Her self-description was right on. Small, almost skinny, short brown hair. Intense. But a happy face—much like the one on a high school girlfriend my mother described as "a blooming rose." Pretty in a no-makeup sort of way.

We had no trouble recognizing each other. There was not only my coat and the crew cut, there was also . . . well, I knew I had a bearing about me that often drew attention. Just under six feet, solidly built, good moves. Clearly on the way to somewhere. That's the way *I* saw myself, at least. And yes, so did my mother.

We went to a corner table at a café that advertised "Food of the World," which seemed to mean Greek and Italian versions of scrambled eggs and toast.

As soon as we sat down and without any sort of greeting, Marti got right down to it. "The first thing is that you must understand and accept that everything I'm about to tell you is what you reporters call off the record—way, way off the record."

"I'm not sure I can promise that . . ."

She held up both hands in a kind of open-palm wrestler pose. *Stop right there,* said her move. "You have to!" She said it with a force that didn't match her size, age, or demeanor. But I felt it. This kid meant business.

But before I could go ahead with a response, Marti Walters dropped her hands and her head with them. When she looked back up at me a few seconds later, there were huge tears in her eyes. Softly, imploringly, she said: "Please, Mr. Gilmore. Please. I need your help. Promise me first and if it ends up leading to a story you want . . . well, we can talk about it then. *Please.*"

She really was just a kid, sad and hurting about something very real. Although I believed in the sanctity of off-the-record, I also knew that there were ways to work through and around it—even ethical and responsible ways—in certain situations. One thing at a time.

"Okay," I said. "Off the record it is."

Her face showed gratitude and relief—as well as purpose. She was ready to get on with it.

"My dad believes he's responsible for the death of John F. Kennedy." She said it just like that. No preamble, no setup.

She must have seen something on my face. Shock, disbelief. Hopefully, she didn't see my imagined headline: AGENT BE-LIEVES KENNEDY DEATH HIS FAULT. I couldn't help myself.

"I know, I know—but hear me out, please," she said.

There was no question I'd hear her out . . . and that I had been right to wear the good sport coat.

"My dad's guilt about that day has made him sick, at first

9

mentally and now physically. If something is not done to reverse his decline, he will die."

Here was what she had come to say. And now she had said it.

"Because of the bubble top?" I asked with an incredulity I was unable to disguise.

"Yes. He thinks that if the bubble top had been on the limousine, then Oswald—or whoever did the shooting—might not have taken the shots."

"But that bubble top was not bulletproof," I said. "It was just quarter-inch-thin plastic."

"I know that. You know that. But Dad believes Oswald might have thought it was bulletproof and might have decided not to shoot. He thinks that even if he did fire the shots, the glare from the glass might have disturbed his aim or might have somehow deflected the shots. Whatever, however, he thinks Kennedy would have lived."

I recalled mentioning this theory at the tail end of a *Tribune* story about the many agonies of Secret Service agents charged with protecting Kennedy. I also reported, briefly and in passing, the counter possibility.

I said to Marti, "Some people also thought it was possible the Plexiglas might have shattered into a hail of sharp shards that could have killed not only Kennedy but also Jackie, the Connallys, the two Secret Service agents—"

"I know, I know," Marti interrupted. "But I want to know what *you* know that might make a difference—what you know that I might use to convince Dad to come to his senses about this."

My reporter mind went racing again toward imagined headlines such as KENNEDY AGENT SICK FROM GUILT. BELIEVES BUBBLE TOP COULD HAVE SAVED JFK.

I shrugged. I wasn't quite sure what she was getting at.

"What did you say at that panel last Tuesday?" she asked impatiently.

"I told the story of Love Field . . ."

"In detail?"

"Yes."

"And the bubble top?"

"Yes."

"Do you have a copy of what you said?"

I smiled, nodded, and pulled a copy of my presentation out of my pocket. I unfolded the two sheets of single-spaced typed paper and handed them to her.

"Read it to me—out loud, please," said Marti. She was beginning to annoy me.

I showed no sign of it, though, asking Marti if she wanted a drink. A Bloody Mary? A glass of wine maybe? This kid was about to jump out of her skin with anxiety. She needed a sedative of some kind, it seemed to me, because all she'd had to drink so far was coffee, with a couple of refills. All coffee was doing was make her nerves—and impatience—worse.

She shook her head. No drink, thank you. Start reading, thank you.

"How about a cigarette?" I asked, taking out my pack of Kent filters and offering her one.

"I don't smoke—never have, never will," she said as if she were the surgeon general of the United States.

Now I had a problem. I had been smoking since I was eighteen. It was a habit that began when I was going to college, went big-time while I was a marine, and was now an integral part of my life as a newspaperman. I couldn't imagine coming up with a creative thought, much less a coherent sentence on a typewriter, without the company of a cigarette. I did not know of a single person in the *Tribune* newsroom or the Washington bureau who didn't smoke.

"I guess then that you'd prefer I didn't . . . smoke?" I asked. That was maybe the first time in my life I had actually said such a thing to anybody—except for my mother back home in Salina, Kansas.

"They're your lungs. Your life you are endangering," Marti said.

I slipped my Kents back into a pocket and prayed for the strength to survive for a while without a cigarette. But for how long? Fifteen minutes? An hour?

Too much was at stake here, I decided. I pointed in the general direction of the restrooms, excused myself, and went away for a few crucial minutes—long enough to take several fulsome puffs from a Kent.

Marti said nothing when I returned, and neither did I.

I went right to the beginning of my press club presentation. "Having just graduated from writing obits and the weather, I was the federal beat reporter. But the presidential visit was happening right in the middle of our major deadlines, so the entire city staff was on the job.

"For my assignment, the *Tribune* had arranged for a special telephone to be installed against a fence right in front of where Air Force One would taxi up. There was an open line to the city desk downtown.

"Just before the plane was scheduled to leave Fort Worth for the short flight to Dallas, a rewrite man from the office called and asked me if the bubble top was going to be on the presidential limousine. It would help to know now, he said, before he wrote the story later under deadline pressure. The bubble top was a question only because it had been raining early that morning in Dallas. The advance word was that Kennedy insisted his limousine be open during motorcades so the American people would not feel he was a museum piece to be viewed only under glass from a distance. The bubble top, which was made of a thin plastic that was not bulletproof, was designed only to protect against bad weather.

"I put the phone down and walked over to a small ramp where the motorcade limousines were being held in waiting, out of view. I saw that the plastic covering was, in fact, on the president's car, completely covering the backseat where the Kennedys would be sitting as well as the middle seats where Texas governor Connally and Mrs. Connally would be, and the front where a Secret Service driver and another agent would be stationed.

"I approached an agent who was standing at the head of

the ramp: 'Rewrite wants to know if you're going to keep the bubble top up.' The agent was Van Walters, the assistant agent in charge of the Dallas office, a man in his early forties, quiet-spoken but pleasant, friendly. Among *Tribune* and other federal beat reporters, Walters was not known to volunteer much information for a story—but he also, when questioned, never seemed to hold back. His regular work, like that of all Secret Service agents working out in the field, mostly involved counterfeiting, government check theft, and similar cases under the jurisdiction of the Treasury Department, the Secret Service's parent agency . . ."

I paused and glanced up at Marti Walters. Her eyes were closed, her hands folded in front of her. She had calmed down and was listening intently.

"Thanks for what you said about him," she said to me without even opening her eyes.

"I didn't just make it up for . . . you know, for you to hear now, if that's what you might be thinking."

Her eyes popped open. "No, I was not thinking that. I assumed you, as a newspaperman, told only the truth."

"Where are you at college?" I asked, realizing suddenly that we had gone so quickly into what mattered, this question about her father's guilt and health, that there had been no exchange of biographical small talk.

"Penn—the University of Pennsylvania," Marti responded.

"Your major?"

"English."

"A special interest?"

"American literature."

"What kind?"

"The good kind—mostly the kind written by women." This, she said with some shortness.

What a great 1968 answer, I thought. A woman—a kid—of the times.

She motioned her head toward the papers in my hand. *On with it, please. Enough small talk* was the clear message.

I continued reading.

"Walters glanced up at the bluing sunny sky and then hollered over at another agent who was holding a two-way radio in his hand. 'What about the weather downtown?' he yelled.

"The agent talked into his radio, listened for a few seconds. 'Clear!' he hollered back.

"Van Walters yelled to the five or six other agents who were at get-ready positions in and around the cars: 'Lose the bubble top!'

"I watched as the agents began the process of unsnapping the several pieces of plastic from the car.

"I returned to the phone, reported to rewrite, and went on with my business covering the Kennedys' arrival and then, over the next many hours, various aspects of the tragedy that had occurred. I was sent first from Love Field to Parkland Hospital, where I was when Kennedy's death was formally announced by a White House press spokesman.

"Next, I went downtown to police headquarters where I became part of the chaos along with hundreds of other reporters from all over the country and the world and law enforcement officers at all levels of government. There was a mix of sadness and disbelief that was beyond anything I had ever witnessed—or even imagined. I felt like I was an actor in a slow-motion horror movie about chaos and grief . . .”

I stopped again and said, “Sorry about the purple prose.”

Marti waved me on, which I took as an English teacher’s absolution.

“Around midnight—nearly twelve hours after the shots were fired at Dealey Plaza—I went to await the breakup of a closed-door meeting in the chief of police’s office at the end of a hall on the second floor.

“After a while the door opened and out walked several men in suits. I recognized one as Secret Service Agent Van Walters.

“He came over to me. Tears in his eyes, he mumbled slowly, deliberately, as if speaking in a trance: ‘If I just hadn’t taken off the bubble top.’

“The words blew me backward. And for the first time, I wondered: What if *I* hadn’t asked Walters the bubble top question in the first place? What if I had ignored the rewrite man’s request? What if the rewrite man never asked the question?

“And so, I, too, became one of the many people connected to the Kennedy Texas trip who were plagued by varying levels of what-if guilt. A guilt that would stay with us forever. Van Walters and I shared the burden with political and White House staffers, Secret Service agents and other law enforcement officers, and all kinds of other people involved in Dallas and elsewhere.

"*What if I hadn't pushed for a motorcade or for going to Texas or Dallas at all? What if I had argued harder to have the lunch at Fair Park instead of the Trade Mart? What if I'd seen a rifle sticking out the sixth-floor window? What if I had reacted faster when the first shot was fired?*

"These were the questions being asked aloud and silently in the minds and hearts of people everywhere.

"What if, what if?"

I began folding up the papers and said, "I went on—to a few laughs in the audience—to tell the story of how I ran out of gas in the middle of the next two nights while going home from the Dallas police station . . . but that's pretty much it."

Marti was looking right at me, but her thoughts went through me to somewhere and someone else.

"So he really did do it," she said finally. "Dad really did make the decision to take off the bubble top."

"But it wasn't a real decision," I said quickly. "The rain stopped and that was it. The weather made that top come off."

Marti, as if a plug had been pulled, sank back limp in her chair. She said nothing for several seconds, digesting, it seemed to me, what I had said and if there was any truth to it.

Her rigid tension abated right before my eyes. She seemed defeated. "I had hoped that your story was such that . . . well, that you knew for a fact that somebody else in the Secret Service, somebody on the White House detail or somebody in Washington, somebody anywhere . . . had made that decision. Not Dad, not Dad all by himself. So many agents and other people have made all kinds of conflicting statements about who did what that day. I have read them all. They're very confusing, and today . . . Well, I wanted you to tell me something that I could take back to him that would make it absolutely clear to him what happened and make his guilt go away forever. I understand from my mother that all kinds of people, doctors and shrinks, have tried and tried with no success. But I was hoping, hoping, hoping . . ."

I very much wanted to take another break for a much-needed smoke. I wanted time to think about what I might be able to give her to take to her dad. But the cigarette could wait. *I* could wait. I decided to open up the conversation and see where it might lead. Perhaps I was stalling, but suddenly it seemed very important—essential, in fact—that I ask her that same universal question.

"Where were you, Marti? Where were you that day?"

At first she frowned, and for a moment I thought she would not answer me. But I was wrong. She very much wanted to talk. And she talked—and talked and talked for hours there in and around the Washington train station and then later in Philadelphia and elsewhere over the next couple of weeks about that day and the days afterward that had led to where she and her father were now.

2

Marti remembered every detail of her November 22. Her memories were remarkably vivid and precise.

I had begun immediately taking notes in the reporter's notebook I had brought that day to our meeting. Marti did nothing to stop me from doing so, a fact that signaled that off-the-record might, in fact, be only a short-term restriction. I was delighted.

She began her story with football. It had been noon, and dissecting the Dallas Cowboys was what Marti and some of her boy classmates always did over lunch at the George Bannerman Dealey High School in East Dallas.

"Dandy is never going to make it—never," Marti had declared.

"Eddie, Eddie, *he's* the one!" a boy had agreed.

Dandy was Don Meredith, the recently anointed co–starting Cowboys quarterback. Until a few weeks earlier Eddie LeBaron had been the starter but now he was sometimes alternating with Meredith at that most important position, with coach Tom Landry calling the plays from the sidelines. "Mount

Landry" was the nickname for Landry, who was famous for always wearing a coat, a tie, a felt hat, and no sign of emotion on the sideline. His National Football League expansion team had won only nine of forty games in its first two years of life, just three of ten played so far this 1963 season.

The conversation was especially heated because an away game with the Cleveland Browns was coming up in two days, on Sunday, November 24.

"Dandy's too funky to call the plays," said another boy.

"Eddie's too short to see the receivers," somebody yelled back. "He's a shrimp, a half-pint midget."

"Can't hardly see over the scrimmage line," another anti-LeBaron Meredith supporter chimed in.

Marti recounted this with what I thought of as tomboyish pride. She boasted that she was in a league all by her female self at Dealey when it came to football details and the Cowboys. She said the boys let her participate in the obsessive discussions because she knew more about the players and football than anyone else. But she also knew that it helped that her dad was a Secret Service agent, who, unlike everyone else's father, not only carried a gun but also caught counterfeiters and protected presidents.

And it was from Martin Van Walters that she'd gained the critical information and the devotion that turned her into a Cowboys fan like her father. On the quarterback argument, for instance, Marti said it was from her dad that she learned enough to remind the anti-LeBaron boys that while LeBaron was only five-seven he had won a Silver Star, a Bronze Star, and a couple of Purple Hearts as a marine infantry platoon leader in Korea. All Dandy Don Meredith had done was strut around as a hillbilly singing football star at Southern Methodist University here in Dallas.

"Little people do as many big things as big ones," Van Walters had said to Marti, not having to mention the obvious fact that he was a small man himself—five-eight, 160 pounds.

The Walters father-daughter pair—Van and Marti being the names they used—were a match. She called them a "proud match." Their full names were Martin Van Walters and Marti Van Walters. The small Hudson Valley town of Kinderhook, New York, where the Walters family lived, was the hometown of Martin Van Buren, the eighth president of the United States. Marti told me that an Albany newspaper once reported that in the years following the Van Buren presidency, more than seventy-five male babies born in the area had been given Martin Van combo names. There had also been half a dozen or so Marti and Marsha Vans, and though neither she nor her father had ever attended such a thing, there were even occasional gatherings of "any and all varieties of Martin Vans and their descendants" as a way to draw tourist attention to historical commemorations in Kinderhook.

Beyond their names and small bones, she also shared her bright dark brown eyes and soft brown hair with her dad. His hair was closely cut, almost like a military recruit's. Hers was short, too—barely halfway to her shoulders.

Her dad had a stern way of talking sometimes, as if he were everybody's father. Marti believed part of it came from the fact that he had spent three years as a criminal investigator with the army military police during the Korean War before becoming an agent of the U.S. Secret Service. He had been in the army ROTC at the University of Albany, a State of New York school, which led to a commission as a second lieutenant upon graduation. Van Walters always told Marti that going from the army into the Secret Service had been an easy and natural move.

As she talked to me of herself, at the time a high school junior, her attention turned to that November 1963 day in the cafeteria. While biting into her tuna salad sandwich on wheat bread, she heard somebody trying to say something over the school public address system. It sounded like the principal, Mrs. Caldwell. She was most likely just making announcements about an old-clothes collection drive, maybe further tryouts for the student production of *Oliver!*. Marti already had a part playing one of the poor grubby orphan girls in the chorus . . .

But there was something different in the voice on the PA. Was someone crying? What was wrong?

"Please, please," Marti finally heard her say. "If I may have your sad . . . sad . . . attention. Something awful . . . something really terrible has happened."

Teachers ran into the room, several of them in tears. They were holding up their hands, signaling for quiet.

"Quiet. Quiet. Listen," the music teacher, Miss Roberts, said. Marti said she and the other students paid attention because Miss Roberts was a gorgeous blonde in her late twenties. In a few seconds the room was silent.

She recalled the exact words spoken by Mrs. Caldwell over the speaker system:

"I regret to say . . . to announce . . . that President Kennedy has been shot . . . here in our own Dallas. He was on his way to the Trade Mart . . . Governor Connally was shot, too . . ."

Marti felt confusion and panic overwhelming her whole being. *Daddy!* she wanted to yell. *Daddy! Daddy!*

As if in a dream, she recalled vaguely hearing Mrs. Caldwell then call on everyone to close their eyes and observe a moment of silent prayer for the survival of President Kennedy and Governor Connally.

But in that silence all Marti wanted to shout was, *What about my daddy?*

She heard loudly and clearly Mrs. Caldwell's final message to the students: Classes at Dealey High and all over Dallas were immediately dismissed. Parents were being notified to come get their children from school.

There were hoots and applause all around the cafeteria.

Marti was stunned by what the kids yelled.

"Can we go now?"

"Yeah, we're out of here!"

"Weekend gets longer—right on!"

Marti fought back anger and tears.

"No! Don't say that!" she shouted. "My daddy's out there!"

But nobody was listening. Not to her, not to the teachers, not to anybody. It seemed to Marti as if everyone in the lunchroom was making some kind of noise, moving around, being part of the commotion.

"I hope he dies!" she heard a boy yell.

A girlfriend of Marti's said back, "Don't say that! That's an awful thing to say because . . . because of so many things."

Because my daddy was protecting the president! That was what Marti wanted to say.

Many kids and teachers knew her dad was Secret Service and was, in fact, working on the Kennedy visit to Dallas. One of the teachers had even brought it up in home room first period a few days ago.

"You must be proud of your father doing such important work," the teacher had said.

"Yes, ma'am, I am," Marti answered. And that was the absolute truth. Marti loved the look of awe that appeared on the boys' faces when she first told them her dad was a Secret Service agent.

She most enjoyed the questions about whether her dad carried a pistol. What kind was it? Was it always loaded? Had he ever shot anybody? Marti usually answered with a whispered, "Sorry, it's all a secret. Can't say a word about it."

Actually, her dad never said anything about the dark gray revolver that seemed to Marti the most exciting part of being in the Secret Service. When not being worn on his right hip in a black leather holster under an always-unbuttoned suit coat, the weapon was kept in a locked metal box in her parents' bedroom closet. All of her dad's suit coats had been specially altered—at Secret Service expense, her mom said—to allow extra space around the hip to accommodate the holstered pistol. The service also paid for the brown felt hat that he wore while on duty. It was considered as much a part of his uniform as Coach Landry's game-day getup was.

Marti knew that Van Walters spent most of his time, between rare presidential visits, in the southwest region of the country looking for counterfeit money and bonds, stolen government checks, and other malfeasance directly related to the Treasury Department. And that was the only part of his work that was available for father-daughter discussion.

Among the non-presidential stuff, there was occasionally something interesting to hear about. Van told Marti about the case of Rubber Stamp Rudy, a retired jewelry engraver from McKinney, north of Dallas, who perfected a rubber stamp that exactly replicated the face of Andrew Jackson and the black print on the upside of a twenty-dollar bill. He used only authentic currency paper from one-dollar bills that he bleached white before stamping on a twenty. The guy floated through a dozen or more Texas towns and several more in New Mexico and Arizona casually making twenties, getting away with almost four thousand dollars' worth of food, clothing, and travel before being arrested.

"We caught him when a small grocery store owner accidentally dropped one of the bad bills into a pail of water and it turned blue from the bleach," said Van Walter to his delighted daughter.

There had been one brief conversation, though, the night before, November 21, about the Kennedy visit and the fact that her dad would be leaving the house at six o'clock in the morning.

"Dad, a lot of the kids at school say everybody in Dallas hates Kennedy. Is that true?" Marti remarked to her father. "Vice President Johnson, too, and he's even from Texas!"

"*Hate*'s a strong word, sweetheart," Van Walters replied with that tone of finality that Marti was most familiar with. "It's politics, that's all."

End of sentence, end of discussion.

So it was only from the comic book *Steve of the Secret Service* that Marti learned much of anything about her dad's work protecting presidents. There was one issue in particular about how they were trained to go toward an assassin's bullet instead of ducking or flinching—much less running away.

And how to throw themselves spread-eagle over a president who was under fire.

It was probably only a few minutes, but Marti said it seemed like an eternity before her mother showed up at Dealey High School.

Rosemary Walters rushed into the lunchroom, frantically grabbed her daughter, and pulled Marti to her. It was obvious to Marti that she must have run like lightning the ten blocks from the neighborhood bank, where she worked as a teller.

Her mother's light brown hair was mussed, her blue eyes were circled in red and streaming tears, her face was off-white—almost gray. Marti was used to the spirited aliveness of her beautiful tanned mother. Now she looked almost dead.

Dead. Before Marti left the school with her mom, a teacher had yelled out at the front door of the school that Kennedy had been declared dead.

And so, too, were a Dallas police officer and a Secret Service agent.

"Is Daddy dead?" Marti asked her mother as they walked away from the school. "Is he dead? Is Daddy dead?" She repeated the question over and over.

Her mother was shaking and sobbing. All she could do was repeat over and over, "I'm sure he isn't. I'm sure he isn't."

But Marti, now also crying loudly, could tell that she was anything but sure.

Hand in hand, she and her mother took off running the last six blocks to their home.

BY THE TIME they ran inside the family's small two-bedroom house between Skillman Avenue and Abrams Road, the phone was ringing.

"Maybe it's Daddy," Marti said as both raced through the front door.

But it was not Daddy on the phone. It was his mother—Marti's grandmother—from Kinderhook, New York, the small town where Van had grown up.

As Marti turned on the television, she heard her own mother say: "Don't know anything . . . not a thing." And,

"Yes, yes, I'm watching it, too." Rosemary had stopped crying. Her face had changed from gray to red.

Marti knew they were talking about what had been said about a dead Secret Service agent.

Their television set, a twenty-one-inch black-and-white, was usually turned on only under very strict rules laid out by Marti's dad, who believed that watching television "emptied the mind more than filled it." His only exceptions were for football and the news with Huntley-Brinkley on NBC or Walter Cronkite on CBS.

Now as she turned the channel to CBS she saw a picture of Walter Cronkite on the screen. He was saying something about how there had been security concerns in Dallas because of previous public demonstrations against United Nations ambassador Adlai Stevenson . . .

Then he picked up a piece of paper that somebody had apparently just handed him. He looked at it in silence, took off his glasses, and said:

"From Dallas, Texas, the flash—apparently official. 'President Kennedy died at one PM Central Standard Time.'" Glancing up at a clock, he added, "Two o'clock Eastern Standard Time . . . some thirty-eight minutes ago."

Was he crying? Marti was. She could swear that Walter Cronkite definitely had tears in his eyes. Marti certainly did. But now she was going to stop crying. Stop it! Stop it! She vowed not to cry anymore—not a full cry. Not anymore. She was going to pull herself together until they knew about her father.

Then the television switched to a picture of the rear entrance of a hospital in Dallas. There were black cars and police cars parked all around. The reporter was saying something about taking the body of "the dead president" with his widow and others back to Washington with the new president, Lyndon Johnson.

Rosemary lunged at the television, switching the knob from channel to channel in a fury, trying, Marti knew, to find something about that Secret Service agent.

Suddenly, as if she realized what was really going on, Rosemary sent Marti to her room.

"Mom! Please! For God's sake, I'm a junior in high school!"

But Rosemary couldn't bear the thought of her daughter hearing from some television reporter that her father was dead.

Marti's thoughts were a frantic jumble. She raced through them knowing that she had ignored, until now, the obvious fact that being a Secret Service agent could be dangerous work. She had seen only a comic book and movie world where her hero father and his fellow hero agents got their man—or protected their president . . .

And then came the magic words from a television newsman—not Walter Cronkite—speaking behind a table:

"This just in. Earlier reports that a Secret Service agent was also killed have turned out to be erroneous. A Secret Service official said all agents are accounted for. The only other shooting victim besides President Kennedy and Governor Connally may have been a Dallas police officer. A report from the Associated Press says that a shooting of a uniformed officer occurred in the Oak Cliff section of Dallas, several blocks from the assassination site at Dealey Plaza."

Rosemary, hearing those same words, threw her arms around Marti, picked her up, and twirled her around and around like she did when she won the spelling bee at Dealey school.

THERE WERE SEVERAL more calls from concerned friends and family before the one that mattered finally came.

"There you are! Thank the Lord, there you are!"

Her mom yelled it one, twice—a third time. Marti could only hear one side of the conversation, but it wasn't hard to figure out what was coming from her dad on the other side.

"I understand, I understand," her mom said, probably in response to her dad saying something about being sorry for not having called before now. "I can only guess how busy you've been."

He must have said something about the earlier false report about a Secret Service agent casualty.

"Thank God, Van. Yes, we heard it all."

She told him that his mother in Kinderhook and her relatives in Albany had called, as had several other relatives, friends, and Secret Service wives in Washington and elsewhere.

"Everybody knows you're safe, honey. You are safe. That is what matters. Don't talk about all of that at the hospital . . . it doesn't matter . . . put it out of your mind . . ."

It sounded like Van kept interrupting her. "Think about you being physically safe. Don't even think about any of the rest—whatever you saw. Remember . . . my mother used to say to us kids, 'Just close your eyes and throw it away,' if there was something we saw that was bad. Well, you do the same, honey. Please, please just close your eyes and throw it away."

After a few more seconds of listening to her husband, Rosemary looked over at Marti and said into the phone, "She's being a real trouper, Van." She paused. "No, no, she's fine. She's so proud of you . . . Please, honey, please. Marti's fine. I promise. All she cares about right now is that you are safe."

After another pause to listen, "Yes, I'll tell her. It'll make her so happy . . . No, not happy because of Kennedy, no, no, that would be crazy. Because you are alive and you are fine—that's why she's happy. I can only imagine what it was like for you, darling. What you saw . . ."

The conversation was coming to an end. "I'll get it all ready whenever you come. It'll be great to see you . . . even if it's just for a few minutes. Be careful."

Then, after another bunch of words from Van, Rosemary said:

"Don't even think that, honey, much less say it. You did everything you could. All of you did. No, no, no. Never ever think that. Never!"

Rosemary kept the phone at her ear. "No, Van, please, don't cry. Please don't cry. Are there any of the other agents around?"

Van said something else quickly and Rosemary hung up the phone.

"One of the agents is going to drop your dad off at the

house sometime late this evening so he can sleep for a few hours," she said to Marti, suddenly brisk and efficient even though the tears on her face were still wet and shining. "He needs some clean shirts, razor, toothbrush, and things. You know how your dad and the agents are—spic and span at all times, no matter what."

"What did he tell you to say to me?" Marti asked.

"He said to tell you not to give up on the Cowboys. Someday they'll make you proud."

Marti agreed about the Cowboys. And then she thought about how wonderful it was that both her dad and Coach Landry wore felt hats. What a very strange thought.

But really, the important thing to her was that her father was not only alive, he was crying.

Not only had Marti never seen or heard her brave father, Secret Service special agent Martin Van Walters, cry. She had never imagined such a thing could happen.

WHEN HER DAD came home late that night, Marti couldn't see or touch him.

She was in bed, dreamily trying to imagine Eddie LeBaron, alive and throwing a long forward pass, instead of what President Kennedy might look like dead in a coffin with his head shot to pieces. The television reports had said over and over that Mr. Kennedy had been shot in the head and with those words careening on a loop in her mind, closing her eyes and throwing it away was definitely not working.

The sounds of the car in the driveway and then of doors opening and closing in the house snapped Marti wide awake.

Once the house was quiet again, she crept out of bed and down the hall to a stealth position outside the closed door of her parents' bedroom.

Marti could only hear what her dad was saying to her mom—much of it in frantic, incomplete bursts. Her mother, perhaps packing Van's suitcase facing away from the door, was inaudible.

Marti heard her father begin to describe what had happened that morning. He said he was in the lead car, right in front of the Kennedys with Akins, the Secret Service's lead man from Washington. The sheriff and the Dallas police chief were also with them in that car.

"We had just turned left onto Elm . . . still moving very slowly. I heard something that sounded like a gunshot . . . I wasn't sure . . . but I said it out loud, 'That was a shot.' Then came another . . . and then another . . . I looked up at windows up and behind us . . . all of us did . . . I thought I saw a guy with a rifle . . . maybe I didn't . . . the angle was down . . . like from that tower at Lindenwald in Kinderhook . . . what a crazy thing . . . to think about Lindenwald."

And then Van's voice got louder as he talked about how somebody said on the two-way car radio to "floorboard it." They sped on to Parkland Hospital.

"It was like a dream . . . going a hundred miles an hour, maybe faster . . . Kennedy . . . was he dead? . . . in the backseat of the limo . . . was he dead? . . . we didn't know . . . the limo was right behind us . . . I could see Clint Hill back there in the backseat down on the Kennedys . . . Mrs. Connally was holding Governor Connally down to her . . . that's all I could see."

Then they were at Parkland. Now the words came like shouted shots.

"Kennedy's head was blown apart! I saw his brains! His hair! His skull! Blood! Blood! Everywhere there was blood! Bits! Bits of Kennedy's head! Pieces and blood."

Then Van repeated everything word for word even louder: "His head was blown apart! I saw his brains! His hair! His skull! Blood! Blood! Everywhere there was blood! Bits! Bits of Kennedy's head! Pieces and blood! You could hardly tell it was him!"

Marti could hear only a few words back from her mother.

"Please, Van, it must have been awful . . . I can hardly imagine. Try to take some deep breaths. You're going to make yourself sick."

Van repeated his line about the president's head being blown apart, and her mother murmured something comforting in response.

And then he said something Marti would never forget.

"I let somebody kill him!"

At that moment, still eavesdropping from the hallway, Marti wanted to put her hands over her ears so she wouldn't have to hear any more. But her arms wouldn't move.

There was a sudden silence. Was her mother hugging her father? Was he crying again? Maybe his head was against her shoulder? Was she patting him on the back? Maybe stroking his head? Wiping tears off his cheeks?

Then, again in a normal voice, Van started talking about Clint Hill, the Secret Service's White House protection detail agent who was in charge of the First Lady. At the hospital, Hill took off his coat and draped it over Kennedy's head. He didn't want anybody to see that awful sight any more than they already had.

"But it was too late for that . . . we all saw it. We all saw it. I saw it. Everybody saw it. Cops, hospital attendants—everybody saw it. The blood, the skin, the hair. Mrs. Kennedy was there, blood all over her . . . along with Clint. Clint had run onto the back of the car after the shooting . . . I saw him back there afterward, holding on . . . he did it in a couple of seconds . . . amazing what he did. Mrs. Kennedy had crawled up on the back of the car. I think people seeing the blood on Clint started the story about one of us being shot, too . . . who knows?"

He said the hospital was bedlam. Secret Service agents, local and state police officers, doctors, politicians, White House staff, the vice president's people . . . everyone was running around trying to make it go away, to undo what had happened.

"Half the people were crying, the rest yelling. Everybody was in charge but nobody was in charge . . . there was screaming about who was taking responsibility for the body . . . we, the White House, the local cops, the hospital . . . what about the autopsy . . . what about everything . . . was there another shooter out there . . . aiming at somebody else, Johnson maybe . . . from across the street. Was he still out there?"

He talked about how a local medical examiner was going nuts, shouting that nobody was taking the body until there was an autopsy. But the Secret Service said forget that and they took the body because that's the way Mrs. Kennedy and the White House wanted it.

"I helped get the coffin and everybody out of there . . . I rode with them afterward . . . just a hearse and a couple of cars . . . with the Johnsons and the body and Mrs. Kennedy back to Love Field. They made us stop at every red light. No sirens, no lights . . . didn't want to make a big to-do because they were afraid to call attention in case there were still gunmen out there looking to take out Johnson, too."

Marti said she could barely hear her father then. He was speaking words but she couldn't make them out clearly. When she pressed her ear against the door as hard as possible, she could hear most of what he said. There were pauses between his sentences.

What she remembered specifically was:

"I helped carry the coffin into the back of the plane . . . God, I'll never forget that . . . Jesus . . . Jesus, darling . . . I was told to stand guard outside of Air Force One—while a judge came to swear in Johnson. I and some others of us stood out there on the tarmac and watched that big blue-and-white plane fire its engines, taxi, and then fly away with the body of a man who we were supposed to have kept alive at all costs, at all risks."

Then after another long few moments of silence came:

"He died because of me! I killed him! I failed! It was my fault!"

Those words crashed out from behind the bedroom door, Marti told me, like window-rattling bombs.

Another eternity or two went by before Van Walters could be heard speaking again in his normal voice.

He'd gone downtown afterward with some other agents and local police detectives to look at a film of what actually happened. Some guy on the street had taken it with a Super 8 movie camera and *LIFE* magazine had already offered to buy the rights for a hundred thousand dollars, maybe even more.

"How can somebody be so sick? To make money on John F. Kennedy's bloodied head? On my failure . . ."

Rosemary interrupted her husband to say a few words, but again she was speaking too softly for Marti to hear.

Van continued.

He had never seen anything like that film and he hoped to hell that nobody ever saw the final frames, especially Marti.

"The man's head just blew up in a spray of red . . . and it's all there in the movie. Kennedy's head just blew up in a spray of red . . . a spray of red . . . red . . . a spray of red . . . just like that. A spray . . . of red. Red, red, red. Red of the president's blood, sprayed up into the air like from a nozzle of a paint can. A spray of red . . ."

Marti shook with each of those words. Every time he said *red,* it was like a gunshot.

Van started complaining about there being no federal law

against killing a president so the locals were investigating the thing—so far at least.

He told Rosemary that he and other agents had been ordered to review in formal written statements everything they did that day, from the smallest detail to the most obvious reaction after the gun went off. He guessed he would probably be sent to Fort Worth and San Antonio for three or four days to backtrack those earlier stops in the Texas trip.

Van also predicted that J. Edgar Hoover would find a way to make it a federal case and turn it into an FBI investigation of the Secret Service.

"Somebody said we're probably all going to be busy the rest of our lives being interviewed . . . interrogated . . . harassed . . . accused. Some of us may even be fired. Maybe we should be. We failed . . .

"*I* failed. *I* should be fired. I should have *my* head blown to bits!"

Then came a shout with a force that caused Marti to throw her hands to her ears, burst into tears, and run to her room and close the door on everything behind her.

But it didn't matter that she had put a door between her and her father's last words. She couldn't get them out of her head:

"It was *my* decision to take it off! I did it! I killed Kennedy!"

3

Marti was shaking. So was I. I suddenly wanted to reach across the café table, take her in my arms, and hold her. Comfort her. Pat her head.

This came as a spontaneous wham-wham. It began from nothing more than a natural father-brother-uncle kind of instinct to comfort. Then, in the second part of the wham, the idea of holding her . . . actually aroused me. The realization brought some embarrassing warmth to my face. Yes, I was a regular red-blooded male with a respectable history of romantic entanglements. But Marti was a kid. She was still in college! I was ten years older—a so-called grown-up. No way was I going to take hold of her. No!

And besides, I was a reporter on a story—even if it was still technically off the record at the moment . . .

I am proud to say—maybe more relieved than proud if I'm being honest about it—that all I did was suggest she take a break from this traumatic remembering. I offered her a drink again, water, something sweet. But no, she still wanted nothing.

Marti had been talking almost nonstop for a truly amazing two hours. I mostly just listened, longing all the while to have had a tape recorder in addition to my notebook. But I was a good note taker. Plus, I had a pretty good reporting-trained talent of being able to retain in my head the general crux of anything said to me. I also took those several smoking breaks to review and expand my notes and jot down a few key thoughts. She had eaten very little at the Union Station restaurant—only a bite or two of the toast and the eggs, which had long ago gone cold and been taken away by a waitress. The only thing she really consumed was a small bowl of fruit salad and a lot more coffee.

She must be exhausted, I thought, and I suggested that maybe she was too tired to continue? No way. But she was in favor of trying to find a quiet place outside where we could talk. She needed a change in scenery, she said. It was November but Washington weather, unpredictability being its primary trait, had turned up a sunny day with temperatures in the sixties that required only a sweater or a jacket to remain comfortable. We had both.

Off we went through the front door of Union Station and within minutes found the perfect place—a bench in a small park between the station's circular driveway and the Capitol Building three blocks away. Being outside took some of the pressure off my smoking. Even on the few occasions when I stayed put to light up a cigarette, I made sure none of the smoke ever got in her face.

I decided to steer the conversation toward ways that I might help her help her father. Yes, I'd witnessed Van Walters's decision to remove the bubble top and I wouldn't deny it, but maybe I could persuade her God really did it. Before I could get into any of that, Marti asked about me. Now she was interested in that biographical small talk we'd missed before.

I kept it brief. I always tried to remember the advice from a college reporting class that reporters should not talk to news sources about themselves. Stay on subject—them.

I told Marti that I'd grown up in Kansas, the son of a small daily newspaper editor and his wife who was—I believed then and still do now—the smartest person in town. She ran the library board and the school board and most everything around that mattered. She and my dad had met as students at Kansas State University, but Dad had encouraged me from very early on to go to the University of Missouri, which was known for its excellent journalism school.

"There was a draft, of course, so I knew that no matter what I wanted to do in the long run, I was going to have to go into the service first," I told Marti, who seemed reasonably interested. "I chose a marine officers' program and was commissioned the day I graduated from MU."

"Why the marines?" Marti asked.

"Well, my uncle was a marine in World War Two. Won the Silver Star. And he always said to me, 'Whatever you do, you should always try to do it with the best'—and the best meant the marines. So it was done."

"Did you go to Vietnam?" I could tell by the way she asked that having done so might not have been the best thing to do—

in her opinion. The war in Vietnam was still going on as we spoke.

"No, I was lucky," I reported truthfully. "I was a platoon commander in the Far East but the war hadn't really started for the U.S. by the time my active-duty commitment ended."

"Good," she said.

I couldn't tell what she meant by that. I wasn't sure if she was making a statement on the war itself or on the good fortune of my having escaped without having to serve in combat. But I asked her no follow-up questions, choosing to leave any talk of Vietnam for another day.

I wrapped up my mini bio by telling Marti I got my first job at *The Dallas Tribune* in 1962 through a contact of my dad's. She seemed almost happy when I told her that my real ambition was to eventually spend my life writing fiction—short stories, novels, maybe even a play or two. Maybe live in Paris. My dreams were mostly about winning prizes for novels, not news stories.

"You're not married, are you?" she asked.

The question, coming from this attractive young woman— kid—caught me off guard. "No, no. Not yet."

"Been close?"

"Sure."

"How close?"

"Well, I met somebody in Dallas right after I got out of the marines and went to work at the *Tribune*. She was a seventh-grade English teacher—love at first sight, all of that. I proposed to her in two weeks and she said yes. I thought I had died and gone to heaven. Then two weeks after that she changed her mind—and that has been that."

"Why did she change her mind?"

"She was accepted to graduate school—University of Michigan. She asked if I would go with her. I said nope. No good newspapers in Ann Arbor that I knew of . . ."

"I've already been accepted to go on to Penn for a master's next year," Marti said.

"So you won't have to dump your boyfriend—good for you."

"I don't have a boyfriend. At least, not one I would want to live my whole life with."

"What's the problem with the guy you're dating?"

"We're in different worlds."

I waited for a second explanatory sentence. It took a while, and all she finally said was, "Let's say he's more of a doer than a reader and leave it at that."

"Have there been others who . . ."

"Hey, enough, please," she said. "I've only lived twenty years so far."

She had a point. And that pretty much ended our biographical small talk.

We came back around to her father. She wanted me to go with her and speak with her father about my exact memories of Love Field and the bubble top. I was willing to help—honestly, sincerely.

But let's face it, I also was still thinking this could all eventually lead to a very good—on-the-record—story for me and my newspaper. It was definitely there in my mind. Hey, that's what we reporters do. I wouldn't be a *real* reporter if I didn't think that way.

And both of us, having taken a major second breath, continued Marti's post-assassination story with her doing the telling while I listened and wrote.

"I KILLED KENNEDY!"

Marti lay awake the rest of that assassination night hearing those words. Her father's words, over and over and over. Her eyes wouldn't close. Neither would her ears. And her mind wouldn't stop racing. She didn't move her covers or even get up and go to the bathroom. Not once. She was locked in place in the horror of the day.

Her little bedside alarm clock—it had the famous blue-and-silver star of the Dallas Cowboys on the face—showed it was barely six o'clock when she heard her father leave through the front door of the house and then a car door opening and closing outside.

He was gone. Her father, the man who said he alone had done something wrong and killed Kennedy, was gone. Where was he going now? To do what? What more was there for him to do?

Marti wasn't crying. She hadn't cried again since hearing those words from outside her parents' bedroom door last night. Her tears, along with everything else, had been locked up tight.

She listened for sounds of her mother out in the hallway

but heard nothing until Rosemary finally said to Marti's closed door, "Honey, there's no school, remember. I'm going over to the bank just to see if there's anything that needs to be done. It's Saturday so I shouldn't be long."

Marti didn't answer.

"There's cereal, you know—Wheaties and Rice Krispies, and plenty of milk, so help yourself," Rosemary said.

Less than a minute later Marti heard the front door slamming. Her mother had left without a word about anything more than breakfast cereal! Not another word!

What about Kennedy? What about what happened yesterday? What about my daddy?

Miraculously, Marti heard the front door reopen.

She heard her mother's footsteps approaching her bedroom. "I know you may have heard a lot of crazy things last night, honey," Rosemary said. The bedroom door remained closed. Why didn't her mother open it and come in to talk and hug and comfort her daughter? And why didn't she try to explain what her father had shouted about blood and Kennedy?

"He's just in an awful state, as are all of the agents who were there," Rosemary said from the hallway. "I bet they all think it was their fault and they are hurting so badly—so, so badly. Your daddy is no different from any of them. That's all it is. They all think it was their fault. It will go away, though, you'll see, because it wasn't their fault. Not your daddy's or anybody else's except that crazy communist fool Oswald. What was he doing working at a school book depository building anyhow, that's what I want to know. Why didn't the FBI catch him as a communist and lock him away before he did that?" Rosemary sighed. "See you later, honey. Everything's going to be okay. Daddy's going to come back okay. You'll see. We'll talk tonight, you and me."

Marti considered getting out of bed, but before she could make a move the front door slammed again. Rosemary was gone.

AND THAT NIGHT they only barely talked.

"What did he mean that he took something off and it was all his fault?" was the only real question Marti asked her mother.

That exchange came when they finally sat down in the kitchen for a bowl of bean soup with saltine crackers.

"It was about something that happened with the presidential car, I think," Rosemary answered. "It was nothing. You'll see. We'll all see. He's just upset like all of the agents . . . you know, about losing a president. There's nothing more awful for them. They obsess on it."

"I just hate it for Daddy," Marti said quietly.

"I know, but put it out of your mind, honey," Rosemary responded. "You'll see when he gets back that he'll be the same Van we know and love."

And that was it for talk about the wrenching night they had just gone through.

Rosemary went on to tell her that the few people at the bank were all still in tears or shock about the assassination.

She listened, murmuring responses to her mother, but what Marti noticed most was the smell of liquor on her mother's breath no more than five hours after she'd left for the bank. Rosemary had clearly tried to hide the smell with mints but this didn't do the job, especially when they sat close at the dinner table over their soup. Marti knew that both her mother and father had an occasional drink of beer or, in her dad's case, scotch when they went out, but there was none around the house. And Marti had no idea that either of them ever had a drink of anything alcoholic during the daytime.

Where had her mother gone and what had she drunk? Had she been alone or with somebody else? But those were questions to be asked another day.

And yet, amid all the questions, the thing that stoked Marti's anger was that, though five years later they would remain unasked, she had been left alone by her own mother at one of the most volatile and dramatic moments in history—and their lives. She was as upset as she was hurt and didn't know how to express those feelings. All she really wanted was for her mother to hug her long and hard and talk about *everything*—not just the occasional small exchanges about food, homework, and schedules.

But she was only fifteen and she didn't know how to ask for what she needed.

IT WAS SEVEN thirty at night about three days later. Marti was in the den doing some English grammar homework when, suddenly, there he stood in the front door hallway. Marti fought off her first impulse—to yell for joy and fling herself at her father.

Instead, she slowly stood up, gave a shy half wave.

Her mother, though, moved to him in a flash, and Marti, brushing aside her hesitation, joined Rosemary in wrapping themselves around their father-husband and holding on tight.

"Good to see you, good to see you," Van Walters said.

His voice was quiet, almost completely without inflection. And he seemed to be only barely touching his wife and daughter. They were doing all of the holding tight.

As they walked together to the kitchen, Marti noticed a disturbing difference in her dad. Everything, from the skin on his face to his shoulders, his walk, and his general posture, was slumping. Van Walters never slumped. He always stood up straight. His posture was always perfect. Secret Service perfect.

And Marti noticed something else strange. Her dad made no mention of the Cowboys, not even the game against the Browns in Cleveland that Sunday following the assassination. Marti had tuned in to watch it on television and heard the play-by-play announcers talk about how this was a game nobody wanted to play, how the Cleveland fans were yelling awful things to the Cowboy players because they represented Dallas, "the city of hate that killed Kennedy." Some fools were even screaming that they should change the team name to "The Assassins."

Dandy Don Meredith had started the game, throwing two interceptions and fumbling once in the 27–17 loss to the

Browns. Little Eddie LeBaron threw only five passes, all of them incomplete.

What made the game even harder to watch were the constant network news interruptions. Marti saw the Kennedy casket, covered in the American flag, being taken by horse-drawn caisson from the White House to the Capitol. Then there were breaking developments about some nightclub owner named Jack Ruby having shot Lee Harvey Oswald that morning in the basement of the Dallas police station.

"Wasn't that something the way Dandy played against the Browns, Daddy?" Marti said to her father as they moved toward the kitchen. She was going to bring it up even if he didn't. The Cowboys were an important thing between them.

Rosemary raced ahead, chattering about throwing together a soup and maybe some sandwiches.

"I'm very, very tired," said Van Walters, ignoring Marti's Cowboy question with a distancing shrug.

He turned around and headed to his bedroom, having said nothing more. Marti had so many *other* questions, too. Where had he been and what had he been doing the last five days? Had he even seen the Cowboys game on television? What about all of the Kennedy funeral and the rest of the mourning? Did he watch any of that? Maybe by himself in a hotel room? At a Secret Service office in Dallas or somewhere else? Fort Worth, Houston?

Marti was suddenly sad all over again—and very scared. *Maybe he really did do something that killed Kennedy?* It was a terrible, terrible thought. But she couldn't help herself. It seemed that something monumentally horrible must have taken him over and now possessed him. Like in one of those horror movies she no longer watched because they gave her nightmares.

Her mother, tears dropping slowly over her cheeks, silently followed Van to the bedroom.

Marti went to the closed door. She listened for a couple of minutes or so before realizing that there was nothing to over-hear.

THE NEXT MORNING her father was already gone by the time she got up and dressed for school. All her mother said, almost in passing, was, "Your dad has to work so the two of us will just scrape something together for Thanksgiving tomorrow. He also thinks it's not going to work out for us to go to Albany and Kinderhook for Christmas this year," she added.

"What's he going to be doing tomorrow and Christmas—aren't they holidays even for the Secret Service?" Marti asked her mother, too afraid of the answer to look at her.

"Taking statements and things," Rosemary replied, almost absently. "You know, working on the assassination—I guess."

MARTI TOLD ME it was time to go. She had to catch a train back to Philadelphia. She was talked out and tired, it seemed, as was the sunshine. I, too, was running out of listening and remembering steam.

We walked together back into the once grand Washington Union Station. The majestic structure made famous by presidents had slowly become dilapidated. Congress had recently passed multimillion-dollar legislation to transform it from a train station into some kind of national Constitution center, but railroad fans and history advocates were up in arms over the proposal so no work had begun. There were holes in the high ceilings, gaps in the walls, and signs and smells of neglect and decay throughout the cavernous building.

Marti and I spoke vaguely about continuing our conversation soon in Philadelphia. She was anxious to get me to see her father, to try to help him come to his senses about the bubble top.

"Could you come to Philadelphia tomorrow?" Marti asked suddenly while we waited in line at the ticket counter.

"Sure," I said, without hesitating.

She gave me her number and a few minutes later at the platform gate to her train we said a completely touchless goodbye, not even a handshake.

I left the station and jogged to my car, which was parked on a street nearby, drove as fast as I could to my apartment in Foggy Bottom, and sat down at my typewriter.

I spent the rest of the evening typing every single word from my notes and memory, taking no time to use capitalization or punctuation. All care for spelling went out the window. I did not want to lose one word if I could help it.

BY THE TIME I got to the bureau office in the National Press Club building the next morning, I had made a decision.

I went straight to Bernie Shapiro, the *Tribune*'s bureau

chief. "It's off the record for now but, I tell you, I am on to a really great story," I said.

I had worked for Bernie in Dallas when he was assistant managing editor. Two years ago he had finally taken up the offer to run the Washington bureau, having decided with his with his wife that their three daughters were old enough to enjoy and benefit from living among the sites and sights of the nation's capital. He had been very involved in selecting me for my job in the six-person bureau. Bernie and I had hit it off, most particularly in cooperating on assassination stories.

"As you know, Young Jack, off-the-record stories do not appear in newspapers—ours included," Bernie said.

"Well, I'm pretty sure I can eventually get it on the record," I said.

"You're pretty sure? What *is* the story, Young Jack?" I didn't particularly enjoy Bernie's "Young Jack" name for me, but he was the boss.

I waited for the magic words from Bernie. "Just between us, of course," he said. "I won't tell a soul, not even one in Dallas."

So I told Bernie the story—in one long lead-only sentence.

"The Secret Service agent who ordered the bubble top removed from the Kennedy limo is seriously ill from a mental breakdown he's had over the guilt of what he did and he may not make it."

"That's crazy," Bernie said. "But it sounds like one helluva story."

"Exactly," I replied. Bernie had blessed me. And I was

thrilled. "I need to go to Philadelphia this afternoon and I need expense money for the trip—maybe even to spend the night."

"Okay, okay. You got it. Philadelphia? Is that where the sick agent is?"

I put a finger to my lips. No more information now— though I couldn't have answered it anyhow because I had no idea where Van Walters was.

4

The lunch-hour rush, if there had been one at the small café near the Penn campus, was finished by the time I arrived from the Philadelphia train station just after two o'clock. There were a handful of student-looking types spread out and about the place, which had the casual look and feel of every college hangout I had ever frequented. It even had the familiar mixed aroma of paper and books, strong coffee, and cheap food.

Marti was waiting for me at a table in the corner farthest from the door. It was beyond the hearing of any of the customers. The sounds of portable typewriters and low-volume rock music further assured privacy.

"We'll talk awhile and then I'll take you over to my apartment, if that's okay," Marti said after a quick greeting. "There are some things I want to show you—assassination kinds of things."

She looked campus-cool in a navy-blue sweatshirt with PENN in red across the chest over a white collared blouse and blue jeans. To my observant reporter eye, her brown hair seemed looser than yesterday—probably the result of a recent shower.

Her sense of urgency was in full bloom. She was clearly fresh, ready, and fired up to get on with her story—but also, I figured, eager to discuss ways I might be able to help her father. I had thought about nothing else during the ninety-minute train ride from DC, but nothing had come to mind.

A waitress came by, and we both ordered coffee. When we had settled ourselves, I began by reminding her that back in Washington she had been talking about Thanksgiving 1963. Wasn't it a funny coincidence that now, here we were, just three days until Thanksgiving 1968?

"Thanksgiving with all the trimmings was not that big a deal at our house in Kansas because Dad always had to work," I said. "Newspaper editors—at least the good ones—feel obligated to be there on holidays with the troops."

Marti closed her eyes, as if willing me to shut up. She obviously did not care about my Kansas boyhood holidays.

After a deep sigh and my continued silence, she quickly described what it was like at that Dallas Thanksgiving alone with her mother. They sat at their white Formica kitchen table, sharing only a few short, insignificant words along with a tiny baked unstuffed chicken, mashed potatoes and gravy, green beans, and a pumpkin pie.

When they weren't at the dinner table, Marti said she spent most of the rest of Thanksgiving Day watching football on television. She couldn't have cared less that the Oakland Raiders beat the Denver Broncos 26–10. Her pro-football interest was Cowboy-centric. Even the 15–13 win by the Texas Long-horns over the Texas A&M Aggies didn't rouse her emotions. But the games helped pass the day.

"Christmas, a month later, was even worse," Marti said, moving the story along.

I pressed her for more what-happened-next details, but she said that she remembered little of what happened in the month from Thanksgiving to Christmas. Her father was physically absent most of the time and, even when he was there at the house, increasingly gone mentally, too, it seemed to her. He seldom spoke much more than a few sentences, and what he did say was nonsense. Meanwhile, her mother seemed determined to ignore that and most everything else that was going on, keeping up a pose that nothing was wrong.

Marti assumed her father was out there still being busy about what had happened on November 22, but she didn't ask her mother about that. Or about much of anything else. That was not the way it had been before—before the assassination. The two of them had once talked and laughed together a lot, mostly about little things that had happened at her school and her mother's bank. Now mother and daughter stayed isolated even when they were in the same room.

A sense of loneliness, silence, and misery was Marti's only real memory of the thirty days between the holidays. Her eyes went moist as she told me that those days had always been full of happy expectation and joy for her and, she believed, for her parents. The Walters trio had never been one of high spirits and loud voices. They were a quiet little family. The only time anybody yelled much was when the Cowboys won.

She said Christmas Day 1963 itself was truly awful. Her father came out of the bedroom in the late afternoon to eat with Rosemary and Marti. The gift highlights were a sleeveless pink sweater for her, an olive-and-gray-checked tie for her dad, and a pair of thin brown leather gloves for her mother. There were no TO and FROM tags on anything, the family custom being that most presents still came from Santa. Marti spent two dollars from her allowance money on a tiny jar of lavender-scented bath salts for her mother and a solid cream-colored pocket handkerchief for her dad.

Physically, Marti said Van looked changed. His face had grown gray and pasty. Between each of the times Marti had seen him—which, as best as she could recall now, added up to only half a dozen between Thanksgiving and Christmas—he seemed to grow thinner and smaller and more withdrawn.

Over Christmas dinner Van barely cracked a smile or spoke a word, other than to recite a Dutch Reformed prayer for Christmas that had been a tradition since Kinderhook days. He prayed this time over a bleak meal—several slices of turkey with cranberry sauce and a fruit salad. It seemed clear to Marti, who stayed out of the kitchen when it was being prepared, that most of the food, including the turkey, had been brought in. A handout, most likely, from another Dallas-based Secret Service agent's family table.

The only semi-drama of the day was the ongoing one Marti

had invented for every meal, however few, she spent with her dad. She tried relentlessly to get him to make direct eye contact with her. But she seldom succeeded. His once bright brown eyes had taken on a glassy, far-off stare, and even his glances were usually slightly off to the side, above, or below where she was sitting or standing. He seemed not to even see her.

Another of her grim habits became counting the occasions when she smelled alcohol on her mother's breath. Marti was up to fourteen separate instances the day the three of them sat down to eat their Christmas meal. She assumed by now that Rosemary had a bottle of something stashed in the house where neither husband nor daughter could stumble over it accidentally.

She felt very alone in every way a teenage girl could feel, unable to discuss with anybody her mother's drinking or what had happened on November 22. Marti had a few girlfriends at school but no real pals—nobody to spend time with after school or during the many no-school days brought on by the assassination and the holidays.

Then, two weeks after the New Year, the worse got worser. The Secret Service transferred Van Walters to the Kansas City office. He would go as a regular field agent, not as a special agent in charge or even as an assistant in charge, the job he had held in Dallas. He had been demoted.

Marti was in the bathroom when she heard her dad, having just come home, report the news of the Kansas City transfer to her mother.

"I was told that 'for several reasons, *we* think it would be good for the service that *you* be away from Dallas proper but fairly close geographically. Also, the freer *you* are of management duties the better off *you'll* be as the assassination investigations proceed.' That's what Washington said."

Her father was quoting "Washington" a person—a force.

The Walterses knew all about Washington. Marti had been born in Washington's Sibley Hospital on September 23, 1948, during Van's first Washington assignment to counterfeit money cases. After that, he worked on the presidential and vice presidential protection details for the next five years, mostly protecting Mrs. Eisenhower and Vice President Nixon. From Washington he went to field offices in Minneapolis and then Charlotte before being sent to Dallas in 1961, a step designed to eventually lead to Van being a special agent in charge.

"He's gone . . . to bed," her mother said to Marti when she emerged from the bathroom. "Hard day."

All days were hard days for Van.

"Kansas City? Do we *have* to go to Kansas City?" Marti asked her mother. It was one of the most direct and real questions she had asked aloud since the night of the assassination.

Rosemary didn't answer directly but said in a mumble, "No telling where we're going next—and next, next, and next. They want to get rid of Van and all the others. Nobody even wants to see them."

Rosemary had said it more than once, and Marti certainly knew that to lose a president was the cardinal failure for anyone in the Secret Service. But clearly there was much more to it than that. Still, what exactly? She remained haunted by that first overheard conversation between her parents, when Van had described the day in such horrific detail. But there was not even one mention of her dad in the assassination investigation stories she scoured in the Dallas newspapers every day. If he had really been responsible for Kennedy's death, wouldn't somebody be saying so in public?

Rosemary Walters left the room mumbling in her distant way, "The sooner we get out of Dallas, the better it will be for us all."

But Marti loved Dallas even if Lee Harvey Oswald had shot the president there. She loved Dealey High School. She loved the Cowboys. And she loved Eddie LeBaron.

SHE SAID THE house in East Dallas was not sold until nine weeks after they had moved to Kansas City. But the Secret Service granted "assassination-associated" agents financial courtesies that included a "special advance payment" to Van Walters for the Kansas City rent deposit. Back in Dallas, a Realtor had stuck a fifty-one-thousand-dollar asking price on the Crestmont Street house, which was great considering they had bought it on Van's GI Bill for forty-five thousand barely two years before.

The Walterses, despite the DC-to-Minneapolis-to-Charlotte-to-Dallas kind of moving around that went with working for the Secret Service, had always bought rather than rented their homes. Van told Marti more than once that it was all about equity, equity, equity, and someday that equity would put her through college.

But this time, a small two-bedroom rental apartment on a street south of downtown Kansas City called The Paseo was just fine. In fact, as far as Marti could tell, there wasn't even any serious talk of buying a house in Kansas City. Her mother did the finding and renting and her dad mostly just shrugged and nodded when told anything about it.

For Marti, the move to Kansas City was just the latest terrible thing to happen in her rapidly deteriorating life. Kansas City had a pro football team called the Chiefs; they'd been the Dallas Texans until they moved to Kansas City last spring. It was something, but they weren't the Cowboys. Marti told her dad, on one of the few times he was home in Kansas City, there was no way she could ever root for the Chiefs. Van Walters, again, barely tossed a shoulder in reaction. It seemed to Marti all he did now when she or Mother spoke, and sometimes he didn't even do that.

Not only did she miss Dallas and the Cowboys, but the move also meant going cold into another strange school, now for the fifth time. This one was at least named for a writer, Henry Wadsworth Longfellow, rather than a newspaper publisher like that one in Dallas.

As she walked into the first classroom on her schedule, her English teacher asked without preamble, "Are you a reader?"

In the most superior and snotty manner she could muster, Marti snapped, "Yes, I can read." She wasn't sure what had gotten into her but so what? "I can write, too," she added. "I can even add and subtract."

Miss DeShirley was the teacher's name. She was tall and

heavyset, an ugly woman with black hair wrapped in a bun at the back of her head. "How anecdotal," she replied in an even voice without a hint of annoyance or so much as the blink of an eye. "I find that students who can read and write, add and subtract sometimes tend to learn more quickly than those who cannot. But that is not always the case. That, of course, is why I used the term *anecdotal*. I suppose then, in your case, it remains to be seen."

Teacher and student were standing across from each other in the front of the classroom, just out of hearing range of the thirty-plus students sitting at desks, a few of whom were eyeing the new midterm arrival while the rest mostly talked among themselves. It was eight thirty in the morning, with the bell for first period only minutes away.

"Can you stand on your head?" Miss DeShirley asked.

"No, not really," Marti said, her confidence now disappearing along with her attitude.

"Can you fly?" asked Miss DeShirley.

"No, ma'am," said Marti, her face red, chest warm—grin beginning.

"Have you read any short stories by Guy de Maupassant?"

"Oh, yes, ma'am. 'The Necklace' is the only one of Maupassant's . . ."

"Always use the *de*. His full name is *de* Maupassant."

"Yes, ma'am. I thought the ending—when it turns out the necklace was a fake one to begin with—is too tricky."

"I agree," said Miss DeShirley.

"But Shirley Jackson is my *real* favorite," Marti said. "There are no tricks in 'The Lottery.' "

"No indeed," said the teacher. Miss DeShirley was now in a full smile herself and no longer seemed so ugly.

"Maybe it's because she's a female writer," Marti said. "They don't use a lot of tricks like the men seem to do."

Marti, desperate for human contact, was on to the other subject in her life, besides Cowboys football, that truly excited her.

"Maybe so, maybe so." Miss DeShirley was now beaming—and even kind of pretty. "Now, that truly is anecdotal."

After moving a few steps toward the front of the classroom, she asked for the class's attention.

"Please welcome Miss Marti Walters to our eleventh-grade class and to Longfellow School," she said in a voice of command and presence. "She comes to us from Dallas . . ."

"They killed Kennedy there!" some boy yelled from the back.

"Kill the Cowboys!" shouted another.

Suddenly several others were yelling things about the Cowboys and murdering the president.

"We'll have none of that kind of talk," Miss DeShirley said sternly. "Marti is one of us and you will treat her as such."

Marti managed only a half smile and a nod before the bell rang and Miss DeShirley began her lesson. The rest of her first day remained uneventful after that.

———

BY MARTI'S PRECISE count, Van Walters was only physically in Kansas City for twenty-two days over the next six months. Only five years later did she find out that the rest of the time he was away mostly testifying, preparing to testify, or waiting to testify. That was mostly in Washington, before Secret Service inspectors, FBI agents, and a wide variety of Warren Commission investigators, lawyers, and finally two of the important commissioners themselves—the diplomat John J. McCloy and the minority leader of the House of Representatives, Gerald R. Ford, a Republican from Michigan.

As predicted, with an even greater push after Ruby shot Oswald, the Kennedy assassination was turned into a federal case. And Hoover and the FBI did, in fact, go after the Secret Service. Her dad said not a word to Marti about any of his testimony, of course. And her mother also barely mentioned what Van was doing all the time he was away. Most of what Marti knew about the investigations came, as in Dallas, from her own eager attention to stories in the newspapers and on radio and television.

With Van gone so many days at a time, there was also seldom anything for Marti to overhear except through the occasional phone exchanges between her parents about logistics and travel plans. When Dad was home the conversation only covered how long he might stay this time and how many pairs of underwear, shirts, and ties he would need.

The liquor-smell count on her mother went up into the high forties. And while she never witnessed or heard him, red eyes suggested crying by her father at least half a dozen times.

There was one hushed conversation she caught just the barest of clues from. She knew it was important when she heard it but she couldn't find anything in the dictionary at the school library that helped her understand. "Sodium something or other that could be administered through a needle . . ." That was what Marti heard Van say to her mother.

Then, after only six months, came Portland—in some ways so wonderful and in some others so awful.

Within hours after his official assassination testimony ended, Van Walters was sent from Kansas City 1,805 miles west to the field office in Portland, Oregon. Again, he was sent as a regular agent—not as a special agent in charge or an assistant. Again, there was no warning and not even, to Marti's knowledge, an attempt at a placating explanation.

The message from Washington or wherever was just, *Go away, Agent Walters. Go! Now!* That was how Marti saw it, at least.

But the Walterses did arrive in Portland with money in their pockets. Because Rosemary hadn't ever tried seriously to buy a house in Kansas City, they still had fifty-four hundred dollars in cash left over from the sale of the Dallas house. Combined with a GI Bill mortgage, that down payment bought them a nice two-bedroom brick house in the Stardust section of Portland. Equity, equity, equity.

Rosemary immediately landed a job as a teller at Stardust Savings and Loan in a shopping center just a short four-block walk from the house. There was no question that her husband's being a Secret Service agent helped her get the banking jobs, including earlier ones in Kansas City, Minneapolis, Charlotte, and Dallas. Bankers couldn't help but react favorably to "U.S. Secret Service agent" cited in a job application or brought up in an interview as her spouse's occupation. Secret Service were the good guys. They were the ones who caught counterfeiters and other money-related crooks.

And Marti hadn't really minded going to Portland—taking another hike into the unknown. Marti's school life at Longfellow High in Kansas City turned out to be empty and boring. Miss DeShirley's English class was her only respite. Otherwise, it was not a great fit. The boys seemed rougher and dumber, the girls prettier and sillier than those in Dallas.

Marti's escape to Portland had an unpleasant beginning at Sunset High School. First, while being introduced to the entire student body at lunchtime, the principal made her say "Let us pray" out loud to everyone in the lunchroom before eating. The principal said it was a terrific way to introduce new students—by having their voices heard right away by everyone. Marti was mortified but then she felt pretty good about how she had been somebody special, at least for a few brief moments.

But beyond the prayer thing, something else happened that made Marti's first day at Sunset different from other first days. After Marti sat down at a table for lunch, one of the girls predictably asked what kind of work her father did here in Portland. Always, *always* in the past, Marti had replied proudly as a great icebreaker that he was a Secret Service agent. This time she said, almost off-handedly, "Oh, he does some stuff for the government."

Marti hadn't realized until then how much her father and her feelings about him had changed.

THREE MONTHS LATER Marti experienced the worst day of her life.

One afternoon a sudden stomachache brought her running home right after school instead of to a school choir practice, where she was trying to make it as a contralto.

She'd assumed she was returning to an empty house because her mother worked until five, and her dad, sickly or not, would be either at his office in the downtown federal building or in the field on a case.

Marti raced through the front door and directly to the downstairs bathroom, which was near her parents' bedroom.

With one hand she grabbed and pushed the knob on the closed bathroom door.

And there on the closed toilet sat Marti's dad. He was shoving something into his mouth.

A pistol! A .38! Dad's gun!

"No!" Marti screamed and, powered probably by the *Steve of the Secret Service* comic books, she threw her body forward with her arms and legs spread-eagle out like a bird.

The force of the collision sent the unfired pistol sailing out of Van's mouth and hard onto the floor while father and daughter slammed together against the white porcelain toilet tank.

They lay where they fell on the bathroom tile floor, both sobbing. Marti had no idea for how long. At the time, it seemed like it might be forever.

A FEW WEEKS went by before she saw her father again. Her mother finally took her through a hospital's main entrance and then down a series of corridors and elevators to a corner room that seemed very far and very out of the way.

She had expected to see iron bars on the windows or something similarly grim but there was nothing like that. There was only, at the end of a silent hallway, a small suite that was tastefully painted in light grays and furnished in blond modern. It seemed more like a room at an upscale Hilton Inn than a hospital.

"Hi, Dad," Marti said.

Van Walters, seated in a chair next to a bed, glanced toward Marti and said, "Hello, sweetheart," in a voice that was barely above a murmur. He turned away.

Marti wouldn't have recognized her father if she hadn't already known who he was. His face was whiter, bonier—more so even than toward the end before leaving Dallas. His hair also seemed sparser, and there was a sprinkling of gray in the scant sideburns. He was wearing a heavily starched light blue long-sleeved sport shirt and dark blue slacks that had a uniform look and feel. So did his shoes, black and rubber-soled.

It occurred to her that this was the uniform for crazy people. For psychiatric patients.

Marti, of course, knew exactly what had—almost—happened in the bathroom that afternoon four weeks earlier. Since then she had picked up enough whispered comments either on the phone or from visiting agents or wives for her to know that what ailed her dad was "mental." And she had overheard the word *depression* used more than once. So this scene in the psychiatric ward came as no real surprise to Marti.

Her mother had her head down now in the hospital room, as if trying to avoid the pain of this reunion—the first time father and daughter had seen each other since the bathroom "accident," as Rosemary Walters insisted on calling it.

Marti gave no thought to reaching out or touching Van. She had a feeling that if she shook her dad's hand right now, it might come off in her own. A hug might cause him to break in two.

She tried to connect anyway—her usual way. "I saw in the sports pages that the Cowboys were thinking about signing Roger Staubach to eventually replace Dandy," Marti said. "They traded Eddie away but I think Dandy's still able to do the job, Daddy, don't . . ."

Rosemary stopped Marti in mid-question with a shake of the head. "Your father has some news," she said.

News? My father who was going to kill himself a month ago in our bathroom has some news?

As if she were about to dive into the deep end of a swimming pool, she automatically held her breath.

"We're moving again, sweetheart." The words were spoken softly, mechanically, and were accompanied by a false, weak grin.

Marti let out part of her breath. In Portland, she was still having her best New Place entry yet. There were two or three girls at Stardust who were fun to be with and helped her meet a lot of people, including a guy named Tommy Johnston, who was cute and friendly and said he had an uncle in Seattle who loved the Cowboys. Marti had gained half an inch in height and had just gotten an A on an English paper she wrote about Katherine Anne Porter's new collection of short stories that had just won the Pulitzer Prize. Her English teacher was noting Marti's special interest in and ability to think and write about those major women writers about whom she had become so passionate. Dreams of literary stardom and genius as well as love were forming in her sixteen-year-old head.

"But we've only been here a couple of months," Marti said crossly. "Why are we leaving so soon?"

Her parents were silent.

Suddenly she felt desperate. "Not back to Kansas City, I hope? Dallas would be okay but I love it here, I really do. I know we haven't been in Portland that long but it's really neat, the school, the kids, most everything. I don't want to leave, I really seriously, one hundred percent don't."

Marti felt she was going to cry. Not counting the awful scene with her dad in the bathroom, of course, she hadn't cried in front of her parents since the night of the assassination. She had, however, done so many times since in private.

Van Walters's face showed he hadn't expected Marti's reaction. He attempted a gentle laugh but failed. "Not anyplace like Kansas City or Texas," he said, finally looking right at her. "It's an exotic place—overseas."

When Marti didn't react, her dad said, "Ever heard of Singapore?"

Singapore?

"Isn't that in China or somewhere like that?" Marti blurted out. "Didn't Somerset Maugham write about it?"

Her dad said: "Maybe, yes . . . probably. It . . . yes . . . It used to be a British colony . . . part of Malaysia. It's an island."

"Why would the Secret Service send you *there*?" Marti asked, her voice now close to a shout.

Her dad looked down and across the room at her mother. Then he said, "I'm leaving the service, sweetheart." Marti had, up until this very moment, always loved the way her dad called her sweetheart.

And so here was another piece of really big news.

With occasional help from Rosemary, Van mumbled his way through the story. He said he had been hired to be a personal security consultant to the government leaders of Singapore, which had just become an independent country—an island nation-state, it was called. The deal was made by a private American protection company that was founded, owned, and operated by former U.S. Secret Service agents.

"But what about the house?" Marti asked sharply.

"The company will reimburse us for any loss," Rosemary

said. "They will pay for private schools there, too, if that's what we end up wanting to do."

Marti hated that "we." She knew that "we" was only her and that "they" would decide where "we" would go despite what "she" wanted.

And *Singapore*? She didn't know if Maugham had ever really written about that place. She didn't even know what language they spoke there. What sports did they play? What were their girls, boys like?

"I don't want to graduate from high school in a foreign country!" Marti barked.

Her mother reached out to touch her hand. Her father barely blinked when he said, "We're leaving in two weeks."

Now instead of crying she wanted to hit something, yell at somebody, throw something as hard as she could.

"The television network in Singapore carries the Cowboys games," said her dad, trying to fake another happy smile. "I had somebody at the service check to make sure."

"We'll be at the retirement ceremony next week," Rosemary Walters said, attempting to soothe by changing the subject.

And Van and Marti Walters, father and daughter, waved farewell without touching.

Singapore?

Only as she was leaving the room did Marti notice faint brownish bruises on the temples of her father's head. Both were about the size of quarters.

She didn't need to even check a dictionary to tell her anything this time. Back at Longfellow one of the boys in Miss DeShirley's class said he'd read in *The Kansas City Star*, Hemingway's former newspaper, all about how the great writer had suffered from bad depression. "They gave him shock treatment at the famous Mayo Clinic using wires to his head for two months," the kid had said, "and then he went home to Idaho and blew his brains out."

IT WAS HARDLY what anyone would call a ceremony.

The special agent in charge of the Portland office, Agent Damon, stood next to his desk, a large flag of the United States on one side and, on the other, a matching one with the gold five-pointed star emblem of the Secret Service on a light blue background. Each point of the star had a word by it—DUTY, JUSTICE, COURAGE, HONESTY, LOYALTY.

Van, Rosemary, and Marti Walters, three abreast, faced Agent Damon and the flags. The only other person present was an agent named Frank Landrum, who was off to one side. Landrum had known Van in DC and had also been with him that awful day in Dallas. He was taller and huskier than Van but about the same late-thirties age. Both were dressed in standard agent—dark blue suits, white shirts, and quiet ties.

Marti felt it was a good sign to see her dad dressed normally again, although the dress shirt highlighted how much weight he had lost. The collar was two sizes looser, at least!

"On behalf of the director," said Damon, who was probably fifty years old, "I would like to read the following letter . . .

" 'Dear Van: It gives me great pleasure to extend to you our thanks for your dedication to the mission of the United States Secret Service. It is only through the exemplary performance of people like you that our organization rises to the performance level that makes us proud of what we do and the way we do it.

" 'On behalf of my colleagues in the service, I thank and honor you for the twelve years you have done your duty as a special agent of the United States Secret Service in keeping with our motto, "Worthy of Trust and Confidence."

" 'The secretary of the Treasury joins me in paying this tribute to you. He notes, too, that a special order has been issued awarding you full retirement benefits and thus exempting you from the regular twenty-years-of-service requirement.

" 'Sincerely yours . . .' "

With his left hand Damon gave the letter to Van while he extended his right shaking hand to Van, and then to Rosemary and Marti.

Landrum moved in for handshakes, congratulations—and farewells.

And that was it. The whole thing, from the opening of Damon's office door, to the Walters family's exiting that same door, took no longer than five minutes.

In the hallway afterward, Rosemary gave her daughter another piece of news.

"Your dad's new employer has offered to pay all the expenses for you to attend a boarding school here in the States," she said to Marti. "That is, of course, if you decide against going to Singapore with us. I understand, believe me, I do. It's your last year of high school. I understand."

Marti glanced quickly toward her father, whose frozen expressionless face seemed to be shrinking, vanishing even farther out of sight right before her.

She had a horrifying feeling that she might never see him again.

5

Marti's place in Philadelphia was a one-bedroom split-level apartment that was larger and better decorated than any student housing I had ever seen for an undergraduate at Missouri or any other school.

"I live well on the guilt money from Singapore," she said quickly, having picked up on my silent reaction to her upscale digs.

She had clearly prepared for my visit, even if it came with only a few hours' notice by phone that morning after I talked to Bernie. Having taken my coat, she led me directly to a box of documents on a desk.

"Here's the first letter I received from my mother."
She handed it to me. I read it slowly to myself.

The worst thing you have to know about Singapore, honey, is that it is hot. I mean, hot like an oven. Hotter than anything we ever felt in Texas. Remember the old saying about being able to fry an egg on a sidewalk? Well, here in Singapore you could fry three chickens and a slab of bacon by just holding them out the window for a minute and a half. Just thinking about going outside makes me sweat all over.

You made the right decision not to come. Your dad and I miss you so but you would be miserable here. I am already looking forward to seeing you at Christmas here or maybe even in Kinderhook, where it will definitely not be so hot. Remember that ten inches of snow we had two Christmases ago! And it was five degrees! I'm sure your dad wants to go to Kinderhook. I don't have to tell you that his memories, Christmas and all the rest, are very important to him. He particularly loved the holiday parties at Lindenwald. The big open fires and the music were always so wonderful. He always got a kick out of looking at the lights across the river from the tower.

Believe me, though, when I say that none of what I'm saying means your dad and I hate it here in Singapore. We don't. The best thing is that it is easy living. You'll never believe it! We have a wonderful place in a tall apartment building that has a swimming pool—a swimming pool!—high ceilings, modern appliances. Your dad also told me to tell you that the Cowboys are on our television, which, by the way, is huge and most of the programs are in color.

Rosemary added a few words about the good food and fun Americans in Singapore and then closed with a flowery declaration of everlasting love and devotion from her and "your dad."

Your dad.

Marti said she hadn't really expected any letters from her father, but she'd thought her mother might provide an occasional news update about him—definitely not about the awful mental stuff but maybe a few details about the Singapore big shots he was protecting. But all she got from her mother were a few totally unimportant passing "your dad" references. Rosemary spent much of her weekly writing space posing questions to Marti about her new life as a boarding student at St. John's School, a private Episcopal school for girls in San Antonio. Marti always answered the letters with what she came to refer to as her "Dear Moms."

Marti couldn't help herself from noticing what she saw as sure signs of her mother's ongoing drinking. There was the occasional wavering line in the otherwise perfect penmanship, and dried spots of smudged ink often dotted the margin.

She also thought about doctors in Singapore with Charlie Chan–like smiles giving Van more frequent and higher-powered shock treatments, putting stronger and stronger drugs into him with needles. And, after some terrifying school library research, she feared they might perform a lobotomy. Would they actually cut out part of her poor father's sick brain? Had her father been taken to Singapore solely so that something special and weird could be done to his head that Americans wouldn't do? Was there anything worse than a lobotomy?

She spent a lot of time researching the Kennedy assassina-

tion. Back in Texas, the St. John's library had a good collection
of Kennedy magazine and newspaper articles as well as books
that had been written, many of them focusing on the fact that
San Antonio had been a pre-Dallas stop on the Kennedy trip to
Texas. The library had the Warren Commission's written report and twenty-six accompanying volumes of hearings and
evidence. She supplemented her reading later with relevant
and more recently published assassination material she found
at the Penn library.

Marti had gone over everything she could find about what
her dad was asked and how he answered the questions of his
official interrogators. She concentrated on what he had gone
through that day and those that followed, paying special attention to the Warren Commission's conversations with "Special Agent Martin Van Walters, U.S. Secret Service."

Now, in her apartment, she laid out for me several pieces of
paper, including this summary of her father's Kennedy trip activities that she had gleaned from the Warren transcripts:

- He had assisted the Dallas special agent in charge in pre-
  visit preparations, including checking out possible luncheon
  sites at the Texas State Fairgrounds and the Dallas Trade
  Mart, the latter eventually selected because of its closeness
  to Love Field.
- He had been told there would be a public motorcade through
  downtown Dallas on the way to the luncheon, according to
  a decision made by White House staff and various political
  entities in Washington and Texas. There was never a discus-

sion to his knowledge of any Secret Service objections or
reservations.

- He had, with other agents and Dallas police officials, driven
the proposed motorcade route from Love Field and then,
east to west on Main Street, through downtown Dallas several times. The main purpose was to clock running times
and potential traffic problems.

- He was present when the decision was made to turn the
motorcade one block north to Elm and then proceed west
because there was no direct entrance ramp on Main to the
freeway that led to the Trade Mart.

- He was certain that there was no reason other than the route
considerations for taking the motorcade in front of the
Texas School Book Depository on Elm.

- He did not have the authority to speak to reporters on the
two Dallas newspapers about the exact route of the motorcade ahead of time but he was aware it had been done at the
insistence of local Democratic leaders and others who
wanted to generate a large crowd to see the Kennedys.

- He was assigned to sit in the rear seat of the first lead car
and keep his eyes on windows of buildings and other possible danger spots.

- He was not ordered to arrange or to participate in pre-event
floor-by-floor searches of any buildings on the motorcade
route. As far as he knew there were no such searches.

- He was not ordered to arrange or participate in the posi-
tioning of armed law enforcement personnel on rooftops or
other high-visibility locations.

- He did not participate in any discussions about the need for special security vigilance when the motorcade had to slow down to make the left-hand turn back west on Elm immediately in front of the Texas School Book Depository.

- He was never informed of the presence of Lee Harvey Oswald, a returned defector to the Soviet Union, in Dallas. Oswald was not on any "threat potential" list he ever saw.

- He did not know and had never heard of Jack Ruby until he shot Oswald in the basement of the Dallas police station.

- He was aware of the recent incidents in Dallas at which right-wing demonstrators attacked UN ambassador Adlai Stevenson and, before that, Lyndon and Lady Bird Johnson. He also knew that a shot was fired through a house window at retired army general Edwin Walker, an outspoken critic of the Kennedys, among others.

- He had glanced at a black-bordered advertisement in *The Dallas Morning News* that welcomed President Kennedy to Dallas with words of hostility but he had not had time to read every word in it.

- He had coordinated with Washington-based Secret Service personnel assigned to the Dallas visit to have guards posted in the out-of-sight area where the presidential X-100 open Lincoln Continental limousine and other motorcade vehicles would be held overnight after their arrival on a transport plane from Washington.

- He left his Dallas home on the morning of November 22, met other Secret Service officers at the Sheraton Hotel downtown, had breakfast with them, and then proceeded by car to Love Field, arriving there at approximately nine o'clock.

- He assisted the presidential detail agents from DC arrange the order of the motorcade vehicles, inspect them for absolute spotlessness, double-check all seating assignments, and look around for potential security hazards.

- He received notice by handheld radio when Air Force One was airborne from Fort Worth for the twelve-minute flight to Dallas.

- He was ordered to help guide the various Secret Service agents and other drivers as they moved the vehicles up the ramp to their positions on the tarmac to one side of where the White House press plane and Air Force One would be parked.

- He, with other agents, maintained visual protective surveillance of members of the public and others behind a fence observing the arrival at Love Field of the presidential party.

- He took his seat in the lead car, directly in front of the presidential limousine.

Marti's summary detailed what Van Walters saw and did after the shots were fired at the motorcade. Marti said she remembered some of that from the conversations she overheard between her mother and father at home that late night after the assassination.

She had searched the Warren papers and everything else for an answer to the simple question: Did her dad feel there was anything he could have done as an agent of the U.S. Secret Service to have prevented the death of President Kennedy?

None of the many official interrogators raised it, at least according to her own readings. She said also nobody even asked him—just for the record—if he believed the assassination was the work of a conspiracy.

In my conversation with her at the apartment, I did some follow-up questioning of my own. I picked up on several of her references to "Oswald or whoever fired the shots."

"Do you think there was a conspiracy?" I asked her directly.

"Do you?" she shot back.

"No, and, trust me, I spent months trying my best to prove one, as did every reporter who ever worked on the story," I said. "There were no Pulitzers to be won by just confirming the official findings that Oswald acted alone."

I pressed her for her own answer.

"I wouldn't be surprised if sometime in the future, maybe as much as fifty years from now, there was a deathbed confession of some kind from somebody who helped Oswald in some way. Drove a car, made a phone call—did something to get the assassination show on the road. A co-conspirator, of even the lowest grade."

I let that stand without comment. Maybe she was right. There might have been somebody else involved. But based on my hours of crawling through culverts and over grassy knolls, interviewing hundreds of witnesses who ended up seeing nothing, and reading hundreds of documents that ended up saying nothing I hadn't already read, I didn't think so.

Marti told me she wrote nothing about the assassination in her brief "Dear Moms," sticking almost exclusively to happy-sounding and irrelevant bits and pieces of her school life in Texas.

Her sister students in San Antonio—the 200 boarders as well as the 450 day students—were mostly from Texas. She had chosen St. John's over any of the more prominent girls' schools in the East partly because it was in Texas. Portland was great but there hadn't been enough time to make it seem homey to her the way living in Dallas had done for Texas. Texas was known for having a lot of writers, and she was also thinking she might really try to work toward being a writer or, at least, a writer who wrote about writers. She did write to Rosemary that a St. John's teacher, as good as Miss DeShirley in Kansas City, had praised her work in the English and composition classes.

Most critically, what she did not write to her mother was that she was working on a master plan to run away from school and San Antonio. She was going to be a literary runaway. The day before Christmas she would pack up a notebook and a ballpoint pen along with a few clothes in a pillowcase and a cache of saved allowance money, walk the twelve blocks to North Broadway—which was U.S. Highway 81—and take out hitchhiking to wherever a life of letters took her. Some of the inspiration came from her having just read

Jack Kerouac's *On the Road* in her Contemporary American Literature class. But there was more to it than that.

She would start by going to Kyle, the small Texas town where Katherine Anne Porter lived as a child, and then maybe move on to Indian Creek, the even tinier Texas place where Porter was born. Marti knew from a map that Indian Creek was more than a hundred miles west near Brownwood, but Kyle was barely thirty miles up Highway 81 from San Antonio toward Austin. Marti had only read in a biography about Porter's Texas beginnings and had no idea if either place was publicly noted. Maybe Marti Van Walters would be the first to create some kind of "It was here that the author of *Ship of Fools* and other great works of fiction was born . . ." placard. Eventually Marti, living off the land of experience and adventure, would go to Concord, Massachusetts, to commune with Emerson and Hawthorne. Maybe she'd hunt down J. D. Salinger in New Hampshire or wherever he may be, hit the road to Catfish Row in California to visit with John Steinbeck, double back for a few days in the North Carolina country of Scott and Zelda Fitzgerald, Thomas Wolfe, and Carl Sandburg, and even go over to Georgia to sample the flavor of Flannery O'Connor and Carson McCullers, and then to Jackson, Mississippi, to search for at least a glimpse of the great Miss Eudora Welty.

The literary stuff aside, Marti admitted that she figured suddenly disappearing into the unknown would get everybody's attention. Maybe even the U.S. Secret Service would keep a lookout for a retired agent's missing daughter—"a gorgeous, brilliant young woman of nearly eighteen destined for the pages and places of greatness."

Despite the urgency of our mission that day in Philadelphia, I was delighted she took the time to go off-message about herself like this. I loved listening to Marti talk, and I had been one of those young newspapermen who bought into Hemingway's advice to anyone who wanted to be a writer: Get a job on a newspaper. It'll keep food on the table, force you to deal with the English language in a semi-coherent way, and, if you pay attention, give you material and characters to use later in your short stories, novels, or plays. The *Dallas Tribune* newsroom was populated by Hemingway wannabes. Our hero was Jerry Compton, a political writer who authored a funny satirical novel about the modern-day retaking of the Alamo by a small band of renegade Mexican soldiers. It was made into a movie with Anthony Quinn and Richard Widmark. Jerry had made enough money to quit his job and become a full-time writer.

I must admit that it was with no small amount of embarrassment—and, yes, even a hint of shame—that I had already begun to think that the story of Van and Marti Walters might eventually make for a book as well as a good story in *The Dallas Tribune* for *me* to write. I hadn't gone as far as deciding who should play me in the movie, but maybe Audrey Hepburn would be perfect as Marti? Glenn Ford as Van Walters?

Meanwhile, on Marti's runaway literary future, she said a "fix-up" fall prom date with a cute guy from a nearby private boys' school jarred her back to reality. She stayed right there at St. John's and after graduation went on to Penn for the next three years.

After our nostalgic digression, she moved our conversation back to what mattered to her now. She showed me a Xerox copy of the one pertinent exchange about the bubble top that she could find in the entire Warren transcript. It was an exchange between Special Agent Van Walters and an investigator for the Warren Commission named Arlen Specter:

Q: Who made the decision to take the bubble top off the car at Love Field?

WALTERS: I did.

Q: What caused you to make that decision?

WALTERS: We had word from our agents downtown that the early-morning rain had definitely stopped.

Q: So it was on the limousine originally only as a protection from the rain, not from a gunshot or a similar violent attack?

WALTERS: That is correct.

Q: Was the bubble top bulletproof?

WALTERS: No, sir. Some thought so, apparently, but it was not.

Q: Describe its material.

WALTERS: One-quarter-inch clear unreinforced Plexiglas.

Q: Bulletproof or not, what effect do you believe the bubble top's being there might have had if those same shots were fired at the presidential limousine?

WALTERS: It is impossible to say, sir.

Q: Could you speculate?

WALTERS: No, sir.

Marti handed me more portions of transcripts from the commission, the press, and other sources about who actually was responsible for the bubble top being off or on the Kennedy limousine. They included those from Secret Service agents who were there at Love Field.

The only mention of Van Walters's involvement was a statement from a fellow agent that "Agent Walters was one of those at Dallas Love Field who put up the bubble top and then, later, took it off."

There was even a former agent who was adamant in several statements that the bubble top was never put up and that he— and he alone—was the one who made that decision.

"That didn't make sense, of course," Marti said to me. "Besides yours, I found statements from many other eyewitnesses who saw the car with the bubble top up earlier while it was still on that Love Field ramp."

There was one in Marti's stack from a Secret Service agent assigned to then Vice President Johnson who spoke in the jumbled way real people often do when they are nervous:

"I knew that there . . . that the bubble top could be used or not be used. And I know that a decision was made, and I do not know by whom because I was not involved in the deciding making process, that, uh, not to do it. There was concern because it was rainy in Fort Worth and there was some concern about the rain. And when we got to Dallas, the sky, the skies, sky, excuse me, skies cleared up and a decision was made. I don't know who made it to take off the bubble top."

A prominent Dallas public relations woman who was professionally involved in the private side of the Kennedy visit said in a post-assassination exchange with a foreign journalist:

"At Love Field was first that I knew that he [President Kennedy] wasn't going to have the bubble, the protective bubble over the convertible. I had sort of counted on it because I thought maybe he would have it anyway, and I didn't want something to be thrown or maybe, you know, a placard to sail out in the airport . . . something like that. I remember feeling a little twinge, and we all talked about it later that . . . whether it became a matter of life and death that day for him because if he had the bubble, it wouldn't have happened."

There was an exchange with the then Congressman Jim Wright, a Democrat from Fort Worth, who said it was Kennedy's decision to keep the bubble top off the limousine.

"By the time we got to Dallas, and he opted for his open touring car, the Secret Service tried to convince him to use a bubble top limousine which they had prepared for him there because of the safety precautions, security. He turned it down. John F. Kennedy made the judgment."

"Did you hear that or did you . . . ?"

"Yes, yes. He wanted to demonstrate his confidence and his faith in the people of Dallas and to be part of them, to share with them, see them, to be seen by them, to look in their eyes, to wave to them."

There was a different—and also partly incorrect—take from the assistant White House press secretary, Malcolm Kilduff, who was to later announce the death of President Kennedy at Parkland Hospital. He said the only reason to have the bubble up was if the weather was bad.

"It was a piece of plastic is all it was. I mean, it folded up into what it was two parts? And two parts that folded up and went into the trunk and all it was was to protect him from the weather. Now, I don't say that the bullet would have gotten as clean a shot through that bubble as it would without the bubble, but you still could have gotten at him with the bubble on top. But the president always felt that the people . . . if the people were good enough to come out and see him that he was good enough to sit there in the open car and let them see him and so he could see them."

Other Secret Service agents in Warren Commission statements and statements elsewhere said various things about whether having the top up would have made any difference:

"I would think that it would have deterred for, let's say, the velocity of a missile coming in at great speed, I think it would deter . . ."

"If we had had a bubble top there would have been some obfuscation of the assassin's view. It is a deterrent."

"It might deflect a bullet . . ."

From the son of an agent: "My dad did remark several

times that he felt that one thing did kind of bother him about events that did unfold in Dallas. He felt the bubble top might have shielded the assassin's view perhaps of the President or it may have possibly have deflected a shot and the President might have been alive today."

Another agent, when asked by a reporter whether the bubble top was planned for use in Dallas:

"That Lincoln, of course, was not an armored car. The bubble top was not bulletproof. But I think most people figured that it probably was. Looking back on it now, you couldn't help but wonder if Oswald would have tried the shot at all because he might have thought, 'Oops, you know, this is a . . . this isn't going to work because, you know, it's bulletproof.' Or the next thing is, if he had of tried, that thing has a curvature to it, and maybe it would have hit and glanced off? The next thing, that thing was put together in sections, and it had these . . . these strips about this size [holding fingers apart approximately two inches] metal strips and that thing was configured so you could have the bubble top on the front. You could have had it on and Oswald could had said, 'Well, OK, I'm going to try it anyway,' and shot and maybe it would have hit one of those metal pieces that helped keep the thing on. So, you just never know. That's something to think about."

The most direct and succinct of the bubble top statements was from Larry Akins, the Secret Service agent in charge of the Kennedy visit to Dallas.

"I was responsible for the bubble top. I ordered it put on

the car when we thought it would be raining during the motorcade and I ordered my agents at Love Field to take it off when the skies over Dallas cleared. Period. Full stop."

And, full stop. I was impressed by two things. First, by the amount and the thoroughness of the work Marti had put into this effort to help her dad. Second, by how good a story this was.

Marti brought me back to the point of this whole meeting—*her* point, at least.

"Were you serious when you said you would talk to Dad?" she asked.

There it was. She had asked with a directness that was jarring.

"If you think it would help, certainly," I said. "Where is he, exactly?"

"He's in Kinderhook now. Near Albany. Dad's hometown. Mom says he's deteriorating quickly."

I remembered mentions of Kinderhook from earlier conversations. My mind raced to Bernie, from whom I would try to get airfare and reporting time for Albany.

"He and Mom arrived from Singapore a few days ago," Marti said. "They're staying at least for Christmas, maybe longer, and I'm going to join them there next week after classes end."

And as simply as that, I was left with nothing more to say other than I would see if I could make the arrangements to join her at Kinderhook.

It was time to go. We shook hands quickly.

I made a dash to 30th Street Station for a late-evening train back to DC from Philadelphia. I figured saving *The Dallas Tribune* the cost of a hotel room was the least I could do on this day of many accomplishments I had made for American journalism.

6

There was a sleety, sticking snow falling with an outside temperature of twenty-nine degrees when Marti and I rode into Kinderhook two weeks later. It was thirteen days before Christmas.

She had picked me up at the Albany airport in the Walters family station wagon, a year-old boat-sized Pontiac Safari. After first thanking me profusely for coming, she talked in a fast jabber during the entire forty-minute drive.

Marti's super-enthusiastic gratitude may have been based on an assumption that I—the good guy who came to help—had paid for the trip out of my own pocket. I was not about to tell her that *The Dallas Tribune* had picked up the tab for the travel. That was after I convinced Bernie to "walk one more mile with me" on the Van Walters story—which remained off the record. It was a hard sell and to make it I had to agree to take whatever time it required as vacation. "If and when the story works out, maybe we'll give you back the days," said Bernie. That's the way it was in the newspaper business.

Then Bernie said something that really got my attention.

"We're talking about something different for you anyhow—maybe soon, Young Jack. Particularly if you can make this Secret Service story work."

"You mean a new assignment?"

"Yeah, something like that maybe."

That lit me up—big-time. I had been doing well, mostly interviewing Dallas-area and other Texas congressmen about what they thought about the current issues and big events of our time. I was definitely ready for some real stories—big ones that mattered.

"What exactly is it?"

"Later, Young Jack. Later."

"Can't you tell me anything? Please? C'mon, Bernie."

There was a beat before Bernie said, "Just make sure your passport is in order." And that was the end of the conversation.

Passport? I had one and it was definitely ready to go—but ready to go *where*? The *Tribune* had only one foreign bureau and that was in Mexico City. But I didn't even speak Spanish . . .

Then it hit me! The White House! That had to be it. Travel the world with the president! Hey, I was ready for that. I really was. The White House! Journalism heaven, here I come!

Meanwhile, I had to make the Van Walters story go huge—and speak loudly. And that meant taking things one step at a time. Marti Walters was my focus at the moment.

Marti's semi-monologue on the drive from the Albany airport was about how her mother embraced her when they'd first greeted each other a few days ago. She held on tightly—much too tightly for Marti, who had come to the unpleasant conclusion that she was no longer comfortable being embraced by her own mother. At least Rosemary Walters wasn't drunk. Marti only noticed a hint of some kind of liquor underneath her minty breath, probably the result of a big mouthwash-and-toothbrush effort.

There had been the letters from Singapore, with their brief "Dear Mom" responses. But there had been only a handful of times when Marti and her mother were actually physically together in the four years since the move to Singapore had happened. Those occasions included Marti's high school graduation in San Antonio and three times when Marti went to Singapore during summer vacation since she'd been at Penn. Those trips were all brief—less than two weeks each—and most depressing because of her mother's drinking and her father's sad, miserable, unresponsive condition. Van Walters didn't come to San Antonio to his daughter's graduation and spent most of his time avoiding eye contact with her when she was in Singapore. They hadn't had a conversation that lasted more than ten minutes or was about anything that mattered.

Marti said she could tell that her father was still alive and functioning at some level. But every conversation she had with her mother about her dad's condition beyond that veered off in some oblique direction. She said Van was still able to work, but when Marti pressed for details she was told that work involved mostly staying in the office to consult with others on how best to protect Singapore's leaders. Apparently he did little or no field work himself. Talk of treatment options led to vague allusions to new medicines and therapies. There were never any specifics. Marti always left Singapore relieved—but scared and guilt-ridden.

When she'd arrived in Kinderhook a few days earlier, it had been almost nine months since her last visit with her family. As the moment approached, her thoughts, worries, fears had been mostly about her dad. What would he look like this time? Even thinner, whiter? Softer? Would there be a lobotomy scar on his forehead, deeper bruises on his temples? Could he even speak coherently? If so, what would he say to his daughter, and how would he say it?

And what would the daughter ask her father? More about the bubble top? The death of Kennedy? How crazy are you, Daddy?

"I'M JUST SO happy you are here, Jack," Marti said to me finally as she and I approached Kinderhook. "I know it may sound strange because we've only just begun to get to know each other . . . but I'm not sure I could go through this without you."

I was grateful to hear that. But it made me feel a bit like a heartless jerk, too. I was proving to be exactly the kind of heartless jerk some people consider us reporters to be. Willing to do anything for a story. But I was still trying to convince myself that as long as I did not permit this to get really personal, I was in the clear morally and ethically—no matter what happened down the line on the story.

We rode through downtown Albany across the Hudson River bridge and then south on Highway 9. Marti's talk, still a bit frantic sounding, was suddenly about trivial things. We came to the Kinderhook town limits sign and then the Dutch Reformed Church Cemetery.

"Good to see you again, 'O.K.,'" Marti said with a laugh, tossing her head in a bow toward a field of gray gravestones on the left. The gesture was aimed specifically at a sixteen-foot-high gray marble obelisk on the grave of Martin Van Buren, known as O.K. for short.

It was a memorial that made for an embarrassing comparison with the dominating obelisk of the 555-foot Washington Monument in Washington, DC. There was nothing in the District of Columbia, not even a park bench or a sewer culvert, named in honor of Van Buren. Marti said she knew from her dad that some wise guys around town took notice of the obelisk comparison between the first and eighth presidents by referring to their local hero Van Buren as "Shorty."

But the Van Buren nickname "O.K." actually had added something permanent to the language. It came from Van Buren's being called "Old Kinderhook" to copycat his political mentor, Andrew Jackson, known famously as "Old Hickory." Van Buren's "Old Kinderhook" was shortened by political supporters to "O.K."—and thus *okay* was born forever and for everyone.

I had already done a little homework on Kinderhook from the various encyclopedias and travel books in the bureau. I knew that it was a postcard Hudson River Valley one-stoplight town, antique and Dutch, always beautiful and cozy.

The only personal memory of the town Marti shared with me now involved a race against an older neighborhood boy when she was eight to the tower steps of Lindenwald, the former Van Buren mansion. Marti lost the race and then punched the kid in the stomach when he tried to kiss her as "a first-place trophy."

Marti stopped the Pontiac now at the traffic light. There were a few stores, a bank, a couple of cafés, the city hall, and the library radiating for a block in the four directions of the intersection. All were lit up with lights and holiday decorations.

Then she gunned the big wagon and resumed her rat-tat-tat talk.

"I was in this car. My mother was driving me from the airport just like I'm doing with you now. Just the two of us. 'Hold your breath, Marti, while I show you something,' she said. Nothing else was said for the next few blocks until she swung onto a major blacktop road, drove for a few hundred feet, and then turned off abruptly into a driveway and stopped.

" 'How do you like it?' That's what she asked me, Jack. 'How do you like it?' "

Marti said she could not see what there was to like. Through the darkening gray atmosphere there stood a modest, one-story faded cream-colored wooden house set back from the road fifteen yards or so.

"I had no idea what was going on, what she was talking about. 'Welcome to our new home. The treatment just wasn't working for your father in Singapore, Marti. We just closed on it,' she said. 'I didn't want to tell you that before. But he needs very special care that is only available here with a particular doctor.'"

Marti said she looked at the house. It didn't have a single Christmas light or any other decoration. No lights of any other kind were on, either.

"Mom said there's a doctor—a psychiatrist—in Boston who is an expert on Dad's kind of disorder. His name is Reynolds. He believes it may be possible for my dad to make real progress. He has some theories that he's working on. He has already been here once to see Dad and is coming back this afternoon. Maybe Dad will be going into a hospital in Boston soon."

Marti then explained to me some of the chronology of what had been happening. She said her mother had called her from Singapore in mid-November to report with alarm that her dad was getting much worse. A few days later Marti happened to see the story in the Philadelphia newspaper about the press club panel that led to her calling me.

"After she showed me the house, Mom warned me about what I was going to actually see when I saw Dad this time. She said, 'It may be all in his head but it's affecting his body like a regular disease. You will see . . . he's not doing well at all. Not physically *or* mentally.'"

Still in the car, Marti told me to look over at another of Kinderhook's Van Buren landmarks—one of the few she knew.

"That's Lindenwald, the old Van Buren place. The one I was telling you about. The one with the tower." I saw the tower with the house, which looked huge, old, cold, and neglected.

Marti stopped the car in the driveway of Lindenwald and finished the story of her arrival in Kinderhook.

"We got to the house where my grandmother and the family lived, where Dad was waiting for me. I dumped my only piece of baggage and raced as fast as I could into the sitting room.

" 'Dad, hi . . .' And I stopped talking and running. I had to choke down a scream of horror.

"There in a chaise lounge a couple of yards away was a shriveled-up shadow of a man laid out under a blanket with his eyes closed. On his head was the dark brown snap-brimmed felt 'agent's hat' he always wore in public when on duty. I looked immediately for a lobotomy scar. There was none. Thank the good Lord. That was the only relief I felt.

"He seemed to move slightly to the sound of my cry and barely opened his eyes. He reminded me of the pictures I had seen of people who had just been released from Nazi concentration camps.

" 'Is that you, sweetheart?' He said it in a barely audible whisper. *Sweetheart.* That was what he had always called me. I was his sweetheart.

"I turned away from him and ran from the room."

Marti put her hands on the top of the station wagon's steering wheel and cried and cried. I leaned over and put an arm over her shoulders and pulled her my way.

"It was two days before I could stand to look at him, my poor sick daddy," Marti said after a while. "We've talked a little but I have still—in ten days—to really touch him."

Now it was my turn to see Van Walters. Almost, but not quite yet. Marti had a plan.

"Let's not tell anybody—except Dad, of course—that you're a reporter" were Marti's last instructions as we prepared to get out of the car at her grandmother's house.

"I can't do that," I said. "The *Tribune* has a policy against interviewing news sources under false pretenses."

"Are you or are you not here to help my dad?" she asked sternly.

"Sure, you bet, sure," said I, telling what I believed—hoped, honestly—was only a half lie.

She shot back: "Remember, please, there are no news sources here or anywhere else involved in this—right now, at least. This is personal."

Personal? Okay, okay. "But how do we explain who I am and why I'm here?" I said quickly.

"You're my new boyfriend."

I smiled. So did she. "Aren't I a bit too old for you?"

"How old *are* you?"

"Thirty," I said. "You?"

"Twenty. But no problem. Fortunately, I look older than I am and you look younger than you are."

That was not true. Or was it? Maybe, I let it go. I was learning quickly that she had a way of getting what she wanted.

"We'll tell everybody that we met at Penn," she said. "You're a Hemingway scholar working on a master's."

There was a lie that I could live with—if not huff and puff about.

ROSEMARY WALTERS REALLY was as attractive a woman as Marti had described. I had a brief introductory chat with her when we got inside the house. But there was an inanimate quality to her that was unexpected. Marti seemed so full of energy and action while her mother seemed completely out of energy and disinterested in action. Also, there were signs of the havoc of drinking in Rosemary Walters's skin and eyes. There was a smell of liquor on her though she was not drunk. I was hit—suddenly, unexpectedly—by a wave of sympathy and understanding for this woman, knowing as I did the details of what Marti had told me she'd been through with her damaged, dying husband. Every minute of their five years together since the assassination must have been a desperate existence for both of them.

I only exchanged quick hellos with everyone else on the way up to the bedroom I was assigned. Marti gave me a quick pass-by introduction to an elderly woman who was her grandmother but to no one else.

I knew Marti's dad was somewhere in the house, but clearly I was not to see him until later.

The huge white frame three-story house seemed to have dozens of rooms, most of them small. Mine was only slightly larger than the cubbyhole I'd slept in as a marine lieutenant at a makeshift bachelor officer's quarters on Okinawa in 1960.

Marti finalized my orders of the day while escorting me to my room. Dr. Reynolds, the psychiatrist, was driving in from Boston and was due in Kinderhook shortly. She wanted us both to meet and talk privately with him before I met her dad. It was much too cold to talk outside and, while there were plenty of private places in the family house, Marti wanted the chat to happen somewhere else. So, on her mother's suggestion, they would meet in a quiet corner of the Dutch Reformed Church in the center of town.

"Mom said it's always open and kept warm for anyone who wants to come in, but she said nobody much ever does," Marti explained. "We should have complete privacy."

And we did. A sign outside told me the church was organized in 1677; the current sanctuary, the last of a couple of rebuildings, had been there since 1869. It was warm and deserted. I followed Marti directly to the pew used by Martin Van Buren and his family, first one on the left closest to the pulpit. On the wall to the right of the pulpit was a six-foot-wide replica of the Ten Commandments painted in Old English lettering.

I was taking notice of the greenery, candles, and an array of baby Jesus, wise men, manger, and other symbols of Christmas when Dr. Reynolds arrived.

Psychiatrists are not the favorite people of those of us who cover news for a living. As an old courthouse reporter in Dallas told me, "Shrinks don't know yes or no for an answer." But the upside is that most of them are characters. Funny, smart, eccentric, flamboyant, effusive. I knew on sight that Dr. Frederic Reynolds fit the bill. He was a perfect psychiatrist, a man in his late forties with a grin, a full head of long black hair, a beard, and a long black leather overcoat. He could be cast in a Charles Boyer movie on his appearance alone.

Marti introduced me to him as a friend she wanted to be present for this chat and, as she did so, I realized that the boyfriend ID was not going to work for Reynolds—not for long, at least. He would be smart enough to realize what Marti and I had stupidly failed to focus on: the obvious fact that it was my Love Field experience as a reporter with Van Walters that would be at the heart of what we were going to be talking about. But I figured we would deal with that when we had to.

After a few preliminaries, Marti and I listened to Reynolds explain what he thought was going on with Van Walters.

"I believe your father is suffering from a form of mental disorder with the symptoms of shell shock, though not fully understood in other contexts—not yet, at least. It is a syndrome, a disorder whose symptoms usually spring from specific horrendous actions on a battlefield—but we now think they may come from other happenings as well. For example, a police officer in a violent situation who has to fire his weapon resulting in the death of a person—possibly an innocent person. That is only one of many potential examples. Your father's situation with the Plexiglas covering over the Kennedy presidential limousine could be another."

Guilt was at the heart of it, he said. "Guilt is the driving force of all human relationships, beginning with man and woman up to and through parent and child, worker and employer, soldier and commander. I may add to that list, of course, the doctor and the patient and just about any other set of pairings."

The doctor spoke in what sounded to my movie-fan ear like the accent of a German submarine commander; smooth, forceful, precise, in control under depth-charge fire.

"In your father's case, guilt itself, through a kind of shell shock malady that went from mind to body, is the potential killer, pure and simple—awful and complicated."

That made Marti shudder and turn away. I felt like I needed to say something—but what? I was caught between being a supportive friend and a reporter. Silence was the only way to be of assistance right now, but questioning was the only way to move the story along.

Reynolds preempted my decision by moving on himself. "We are beginning, I believe, to expand our understanding of this kind of terrible result of a guilt that is so pathological, it leads to physical disease."

"They gave Dad drugs and shocked him with a machine, didn't they?" Marti suddenly barked at the doctor.

"I am not privy to all of the prior treatment protocols that were used on your father," the doctor said. "But based on my examination of him, I would say there are definite signs that he has undergone extensive electroshock treatment."

"I saw those scars on his temples from the very beginning," Marti said. "I hate it that they've done that."

"There are perfectly legitimate and constructive uses for electroshock treatments for some patients in some situations," Reynolds said, perhaps trying to reassure her.

"What medicines have they given him?"

"Mostly a barbiturate, Sodium Pentothal."

"Tell me about Sodium Pentothal," Marti demanded.

Reynolds, smiling and patient, said: "Technically called thiopental, it became the first of the really popular anesthetic drugs for animals. In humans, it was mostly prescribed for minor or short-term purposes such as cesarean section births. But with different dosages and combinations it is used for all kinds of things including a truth serum. The psychiatric use, quite simply, has been to calm people down enough to help them recall experiences or memories they may have repressed."

"LSD?" I asked. "I read where some psychiatrists are experimenting with LSD on Vietnam vets—those having serious mental problems. Is that right?"

Reynolds only got half a sentence out: "That is true—"

"That would make him really crazy! Do not let anybody give my dad LSD!" Marti's voice was somewhere between a marine DI and a hysterical child. "Did they already do that in Singapore?"

"I don't believe so," Reynolds said calmly.

"What about psychiatric therapy, with or without drugs—trying to talk it out of him?" Marti asked. "Have they tried that on Dad?"

"Yes. That's been prescribed and utilized more than once."

"Did it do any good?"

Reynolds shook his head. "His situation has continued to worsen."

"They gave him a lobotomy in Singapore, didn't they?"

Reynolds moved his head slightly. "No, they did not. In fact, I understand it was a move toward such a possibility that caused your mother to bring your father back here from Singapore."

"Are you sure they didn't?" Marti persisted.

"Certain," Reynolds said. "There would be a cutting scar right down the center of his forehead if such a thing had been done."

Marti sat back down in a defeated slump. End of attack mode—for now. "You know, Mom has problems herself but she definitely made the right decision to get him out of there."

She had directed that to me. "It certainly seems that way to me—yes," I responded.

To Reynolds, Marti said: "Even without a lobotomy, they've almost killed him, haven't they? With drugs and electricity. Put him at death's door. He is dying."

Reynolds ignored that. "The important point is that I am involved now at your mother's request. I am trying to develop new forms of treatment for your father and others similarly afflicted. There is an escalating effort because of the war in Vietnam and the casualties of the mind it is producing . . ."

"What kind of new treatments? No LSD, right?"

"No LSD—not from me, I can assure you. My interest is in approaches that get the patient to relive the experience that caused the trauma in the first place but with the goal of reaching a different result. I am interested in possibly even employing various forms of reenactment."

Marti looked at me. She nodded, a signal for me to go ahead. *Tell him. Tell him about the ramp and the bubble top. Tell him you're a reporter. It's okay. Do it.*

And I did.

When I finished my full story, Reynolds said, "First, let me understand that we are talking here on a confidential basis and that you are not functioning as a journalist or anything remotely similar to such a thing?" He spit out the term *journalist* as if it were comparable to *serial killer*—or a particularly severe new strain of venereal disease.

That is so, I semi-lied.

"So you are telling me that you are prepared to attempt a reenactment of Agent Walters's and your specific actions that day concerning the removal of the plastic covering?" There was now a hint of positive excitement in Reynolds's voice.

I told him I was.

"Excellent," said the doctor. I was no longer a crook or a scourge—temporarily, at least. "That is excellent."

"Will this cure him? Will this bring him back to life?" Marti asked.

"There is no sure answer to that question at this point," Reynolds said. "But we are going to try our best—that is all that can be said."

Reynolds and I discussed in detail how I should go about reliving the most traumatic experience of Van Walters's life and, in a much smaller way, my own.

Finally, Marti, her energy and spark now long gone, asked: "Doctor, are there mental disorders that . . . well, are like cancer? There are treatments galore but, in the end, no cures?"

Reynolds showed some real stuff with his answer, I thought. "Yes, there are. I wish there weren't but wishing has never cured anything, including certain types of cancer of the mind as well as the body."

In different circumstances among three different people that might have been a natural prelude for a quick kneeling at the altar of the Dutch Reformed Church of Kinderhook. But nobody offered a prayer for Martin Van Walters. The only one who knelt was Reynolds. He went from his chair to Marti on the pew next to me, took both of her hands, and said: "Miss Walters, in a professional sense, if your father dies it will be over my very own dead body."

I laughed. It was actually a very funny line. Marti smiled as she blew her nose in a handkerchief.

"Well, then, let's get on with it," she said as she stood up, ready to get on with it—right now.

I BARELY RECOGNIZED Van Walters. His physical appearance was much worse than Marti's descriptions and anything I had imagined. He was a shadow, a ghost, a small piece of the man I had known five years ago as the assistant agent in charge of the Dallas office of the United States Secret Service.

He wore a short-sleeved dark blue shirt, his skin gray and loose, his bones on the verge of protruding from his cheeks, hands, and arms. He was lying, fetal, on a chaise lounge. A heavy red college-initialed blanket covered him from the chest on down. The felt agent's hat Marti had mentioned was on a table beside him. His bare head displayed no lobotomy scar, only the traces of the shock treatments on his temples. A few strands of hair, silken thin and white, were all that was left on his head.

I knew for a fact that this man was forty-two years old. But based on what I was seeing with my own two eyes I would have sworn that he was at least a hundred. Marti's assertion that he was dying or near death seemed suddenly an understatement. The miracle was that this achingly sad figure was still breathing.

"Dad!" Marti said to him sharply. "Dad! There's somebody here to see you!"

Van Walters's body—I figured it couldn't weigh much more than 120 pounds—trembled slightly. He raised his head and tried to open his eyes.

"Look at him, Dad! You might remember him!"

I leaned forward as far as I could without touching him. His breath was sour. I could see his eyes up in the sockets trying to focus on me as his daughter had ordered him.

"I'm Jack Gilmore. The reporter for *The Dallas Tribune*," I said.

He frowned. It was slight and quick. But it proved that Van Walters was, in fact, still alive. All it took to rouse him was to mention that I was with *The Dallas Tribune*.

Marti motioned for me to continue—to get on with it.

"I was at Love Field that day. I was the one who asked you about the bubble top. Do you remember?"

His eyes clicked wide open. "Yes," he said in a weak voice.

"I talked about how rewrite wanted to know if the bubble was going to be up during the motorcade . . ."

Van Walters stopped me. He did so with a quick wave of his right hand. I barely saw it. But he was signaling that he didn't need to hear all that. He remembered.

"If I hadn't asked the question maybe it would not have been taken off the car," I said, getting down to the real business.

"Wrong," Walters said with a little more force than his yes. "I . . . killed . . . Kennedy."

"No, sir. That is not true."

"The . . . order to take it down . . . I gave . . . it." The words came slowly—but they were coming. He was growing in strength before my very eyes.

"Doesn't matter," I said with as much authority as I could muster. "The shots would have probably shattered the bubble top and everybody would have been killed. Mrs. Kennedy, the Connallys."

"A theory . . . not . . . never proven." He stopped talking. Then, after taking a couple of breaths, he said, still haltingly but firmly, "Nobody . . . no . . . body . . . ever did any . . . tests . . . about that." Another pause. "Did they?"

I had to agree with him. "No, not that I know of."

Marti gave me an agitated, disappointed look. Did she want me to lie about it? Say, yeah, sure, there was a test of the shattered glass idea? Well, forget it. No way, Miss Walters. I may spin and evade but I will not lie—not even for you.

I stayed on the course that Reynolds had laid out in our conversation at the church.

"There is one thing that we could do that might be helpful, Agent Walters," I said.

"No more . . . not an agent anymore."

"All right, sir. *Mister* Walters. We could—you and I—relive, reenact what we did at Love Field that day."

I could tell there was a reaction in Van Walters's body as well as his mind. So could Marti. Tears of joy—real, incredible joy—were forming in her eyes.

"Why? Why . . . would we want to do that?" Van Walters asked.

"Maybe, who knows, something could trigger new thoughts for you, sir. Maybe you would see it all differently so that it could make a difference in the way you have reacted to the Kennedy tragedy. It could lead to some healing."

Walters closed his eyes and laid his head back. He seemed simultaneously defeated and stronger as he said with no breaks or pauses: "I don't think that is possible. You're not doing a newspaper story about what's happened to me are you?"

Damn. "No, sir," I semi-lied. "I'm here because your daughter asked me to come. She read something in the paper about what I said about you and me at Love Field and the bubble top."

"Why and where did you say it?"

"At a Kennedy assassination anniversary panel discussion."

"What anniversary?"

"The fifth."

Walters's head came up off the back of the chaise. His eyes went wet. "Five years since I killed him? I cannot believe it."

"You did not kill him, sir. You really didn't. Let's do the reenactment."

Now we were at nut-cutting time. He either got up on his feet, so to speak, or not.

"Waste of time," said Walters, his voice still gaining strength. "Won't prove a thing. I know what I did. Doing it again isn't going to change anything."

"Please give it a try. That's all I ask."

"Why do you care about me, Mr. Reporter?"

Great question, sir, I wanted to say. I wanted to tell him that maybe I care because . . . well, because I feel a part of the events that have led to your terrible sickness. I care because . . . well, I've developed a do-what-she-wants fondness of sorts for your daughter who is ten years younger than me. And I care because . . . well, what's happened to you has the makings of one helluva story not only for *The Dallas Tribune* but for, as they used to say in the newspaper business, the world and all ships at sea.

What I said was, "I feel a part of what happened and I want to see if I can help you."

That must have rung some kind of bell because he gave a head motion to Marti to give him a hand. A hand to help him stand up. A hand to help him do what this reporter wanted.

She was delighted and so was I.

Marti didn't weigh much more than her father but she and I, working on both shoulders and arms, managed to get the dangerously frail man to his feet.

We helped him take a few steps forward, away from the chaise lounge. He steadied himself. I moved backward so I was still facing him.

"All right, sir, remember, I said what I did about re-write . . ."

"No need to go through that."

"Okay, you looked up into the sky . . . right?"

"Right." He turned his head upward slightly and then right back down.

"Remember what you said?" I pressed.

" 'Looks clear' . . . that's what I said. Something like that."

"Then what did you do?"

"I turned back to the other agents down the ramp."

"That's right. I listened to you say something to one of them . . ."

" 'Check if it's clear downtown.' That's what I said."

"Exactly. And the agent talked into a handheld two-way radio . . ."

"That was Ed Ellison. He was on the White House detail."

I waited for Walters to finish the story on his own. He remained standing—but silent.

So I said: "'All clear downtown!' Isn't that what Agent Ellison said?"

Van Walters nodded.

Now we were there—at the moment that mattered.

I did not want to prompt him any further. Reynolds had said at our church meeting that the key was to get Walters to repeat on his own as much of his words and actions as possible.

Seconds of silence went by. Marti was anxious—ready to do some prompting if necessary, it seemed. I signaled with a quick shake of my head not to say a word. Don't interfere.

It seemed an eternity but it was probably only thirty or forty seconds.

I felt I had to make the final push. "Please say what it is you said then to the other agents."

Van Walters, still on his feet, was staring off in space beyond me. I thought maybe he was seeing things out there— possibly the exact scene at the top of that Love Field ramp.

"Say it," I said again, this time in not much more than a loud whisper. "Just go ahead and say it, sir."

"'Lose the bubble top!' That's what I said." His voice was still weak, but there was no question that Van Walters was recreating his yell from November 22, 1963.

Marti was bawling. It took almost everything I had not to do so myself. I felt a great sense of accomplishment.

Then, with no help from either of us, Walters returned to

the chaise lounge, sat down, stretched out on it, and closed his eyes as if nothing at all had happened.

Dr. Reynolds and Rosemary Walters, both of whom had been watching and listening through cracks in doors from adjoining rooms, came rushing in.

Rosemary leaned down and kissed her husband on the cheek.

"Well done, Mr. Walters," Reynolds said. "I think you have taken a giant step toward recovery."

Van Walters made no sign or noise of response.

"Dad," Marti said. "We could be on our way somewhere good . . ."

"No, I don't think so," said her father. "All your gentleman reporter friend and I have done is proven that I made the decision that ended up killing the president. The fact remains and will always remain that if the bubble top had been on that limo, Kennedy would have not died."

IT WAS AS ice-cold up in my little cubbyhole room as it was outside. If heat from a furnace or anything else was supposed to rise up that far into the old house, it had failed to do so. The bare wooden floor with its frigid temperature gave the room the feel of a meat locker. (And I knew about meat lockers. I was in one once with Dallas sheriff's deputies checking out the body of a cheating gambler who'd been stored there after having had his throat cut.)

Shivering, I quickly got ready for bed and climbed under the several layers of covers on the double bed—three wool blankets of various colors and designs, a flowered quilt, a heavy white sheet on the bottom, and an olive-green bedspread on top. That all made for quite a load, but it felt good and I was warmer within minutes. There was a smell of soap and mothballs that reminded me of my parents' seldom-used guest bedroom back home in Kansas.

I was just about to switch off the lamp on the bedside table when there she was. Marti.

She was tiptoeing through my door wearing a pair of white furry slippers and a large flannel robe that hung down to the floor. I had no idea what she was wearing underneath the robe. It was an immediate thought I just couldn't help.

"Hi, Jack," she said.

It was a scene that I had witnessed in the movies but never before in real life. I had occasionally imagined such a happening—a beautiful young woman slipping into my room unbidden and unannounced . . . But it had never happened. Not until right now . . . this very moment.

"Well . . . hi," I replied.

"May I?" she said, grabbing the covers and scooting in under them next to me. I had no problem making room for her.

So much, I thought, for my rule against sleeping with sources. So much for a lot of things . . .

But she did not reach out and grab me. I didn't do that to her, either.

"Don't get the wrong idea," she said matter-of-factly. "But

it's too cold for me to sit down on that big old pillow over there in the corner. And we need to talk about what we do next." Her head and eyes pointed toward the ceiling, which I knew—because I was doing the same thing myself—was nothing more than a blank expanse of plaster.

We had ended our evening downstairs with a long post-ramp-reenactment discussion with Marti's mother and Reynolds.

Reynolds had tried his best to put a good face on the failure of the reenactment to trigger anything at all in Van Walters. The truth was, it really hadn't done what we all hoped it would do. Yes, he did actually speak clearly and responsively and get up on his feet, but that was as far as it went. For Van Walters there was no new way to look at what he had done on November 22, 1963. Reynolds said he would make arrangements for Walters to come to Boston for hospitalized in-patient treatment the next day.

"What kind of treatment?" Marti had asked. "Not drugs. No LSD, right?"

"Definitely not. But beyond that I'm not sure: a therapy of a specific nature still to be determined," said Reynolds, an honest man. "To leave him here in this condition while he continues to fade away . . . well, that is unacceptable, is it not?"

Marti and her mother agreed.

I knew that Marti was probably recalling the same thing I was—Reynolds's earlier analogy with cancer as a malady beyond cure.

But we didn't talk about it. Not then.

Before going up to my cold bed, I had some white wine and a supper of beef stew and green salad with Marti and her mother. There was no conversation about anything that mattered. Nobody had the energy to talk anymore about the man in the room down the hall and his prognoses.

It had been a long, hard, disappointing day. And now, here in bed, it wasn't over yet.

What do we do next?

I had no answer to Marti's question. And I am not proud to say what I was thinking. As a helper, I had done my best. As a reporter, I had my story. Van Walters, the Secret Service agent who ordered the bubble top taken off the presidential limo, was dead—or about to die—because he believed he was responsible for the death of President John F. Kennedy. Period. "Thirty," as they said in the newspaper business.

"What kind of marine were you?" Marti asked from her position next to me in bed. She looked at me, but still there was no touching.

She caught me off guard. "A damn good one," I said, having no idea where this was going. Stupid me.

"Did you learn to shoot a rifle?"

"Absolutely. I qualified on the rifle range as an expert each of the three years I was on active duty."

"Are you as good a shot as Oswald?"

"Better . . ." Whoops. Still mostly eyeing just the ceiling, I said, "What in the hell are you thinking?"

Everything in the bed and the room went from cold to hot.

"What about trying another kind of reenactment? A real one?" Marti said as she turned to face me and a hand fell loosely on my shoulder. Her knee touched mine.

"Let's talk about it in the morning," I said, making no reciprocal move.

"But what if we could prove to Dad that the rifle shots would have shattered that Plexiglas and killed everyone? That would do it. It *might* do it. Isn't it worth a try?"

I was now thinking intently about not sleeping with a source, a rather loose unofficial rule in the world of *The Dallas Tribune* and American journalism. I had particularly resolved never to do such a thing after the Kennedy assassination over my annoyance with a reporter from a competing newspaper who made no secret of doing so in the interest of "cultivating sources." (I will let the details lie—to protect the guilty.)

But I knew if I did not get Marti Walters out of this bed and away from me right now . . .

"You're a college girl and I really am ten years older than you are," I said, jerking the covers off me and moving to jump out of bed.

"This is the sixties, for God's sake," Marti said, on the verge of laughing. "I thought marines were . . . well, marines."

I was now standing on the floor, my feet instantly turning icy cold.

"Promise to think about it," she said, making her own move to get out on the other side of the bed.

"Think about what?"

"Reenacting Oswald shooting at Kennedy with the bubble top *on* the car."

"Okay, okay, I promise."

She slipped out of my bed, pranced to the door, and disappeared.

I returned to bed with thoughts that had nothing to do with reenacting, bubble tops, or rifle shots. I was busy—ever so busy—imagining, in detail, something else entirely.

7

I walked right up to a young sergeant in dress blues and spit shines at the marine recruiting station in Albany. He was seated at the first desk in the room.

"I am a former marine and I need some help," I said, having marched in unannounced and most uncomfortable.

Marti had driven me here to the downtown federal building. She planned to park in a lot across the street and go to a pay phone at a café nearby to make some phone calls about Plexiglas.

The marine sergeant in front of me, in his late twenties, looked like he had stepped right off a recruiting poster. He had a close-cropped warrior haircut, a solid build, and an upright bearing. I glanced at the ribbons over the left pocket of his dark blue tunic and was most impressed. He had been awarded the Bronze Star with a V for valor and a Purple Heart for his wounds—clearly from duty in Vietnam. It made me want to apologize for not having seen combat and then just get the hell out of there.

But it was too late for that. He had jumped to his feet, his face lighting up, when I first appeared, obviously having thought he had a live one—a walk-in volunteer ready to go fight the commies in Vietnam.

"I'm Lambert—Sergeant Greg Lambert—have a seat, sir," he said after hearing my opening line. "Tell me about yourself."

The young sergeant had lost some of his live-one enthusiasm as soon as he realized I was no recruit, but the smile was there. I was at the recruiting office because, after a morning of heavy talk with Marti, this was the only place I could think of to go. I had no way to acquire a high-powered rifle on my own. Marti said she would take care of the facsimile bubble top search. Sure. Good luck with that. I thought I was just going through the motions, to be honest.

"I always believed marines could do anything," Marti had said, at the end of our very tough conversation about the whole thing.

I had begun by saying no. No way. I would not participate in any such reenactment exercise. Even if we—I—could somehow arrange it, the end result might be just the opposite of what she wanted.

"What if it doesn't shatter?" I said maybe fifty times. "What if the bullets are deflected? What if we prove your dad is right to believe the bubble top might really have saved Kennedy's life?"

Her argument back was always the same. "What do we have to lose? Dad is going to die if something isn't done by us, Dr. Reynolds, or some unknown god out there."

Reluctantly, most reluctantly, I agreed to at least try to see what could be done. I knew that I was being further sucked in to—to what I didn't know, exactly. I was careful not to think the scenario all the way through to any definitive conclusion.

Now with young marine sergeant Lambert, before laying out my request for help, I responded to the request to tell him about myself. I said I had been on active duty from 1959 to '62 and, for good measure, I showed him my reserve ID card, which had my photo and rank as first lieutenant. I was in the so-called Ready Reserve—ready to go if called but with no ongoing responsibility to attend meetings or organized activities. I said nothing about being a newspaperman.

"What outfit were you in, Lieutenant?"

"One-Nine," I said, marine talk for the First Battalion Ninth Marine Regiment of the Third Marine Division.

"They had a rough time at Khe Sanh, sir."

I had heard about that. I had known several marines who were there. What they went through was so rough, in fact, that One-Nine drew the permanent nickname of "the Walking Dead." Having already given him my active-duty dates, I did not have to underline the obvious—and embarrassing—fact that, unlike him, I had not been in combat.

"You, Sergeant? Your outfit?"

"Most of my time at 'Nam was in Two-Five," said Lambert. Two-Five was an infantry battalion in the First Division.

I made some stupid comment about how tough it had been and still was for all marines in Vietnam, which the sergeant acknowledged. Then he turned the attention back to me.

125

"You said you needed some help, sir. You know what we say in the corps. 'The difficult will be done immediately, the impossible will take a little longer.' What can I do for you?"

I knew I was about to ask this young marine to do something that was definitely difficult and, most likely, impossible. I had warned Marti that I might very well draw outright refusal, if not ridicule. I told her the marines of Albany might even turn me over to local police or mental health professionals for even suggesting such a crazy thing.

But here I went: "Sergeant, it's a long and involved story but, to get right to the point—I want to create an experiment involving the assassination of President Kennedy."

The sergeant's pleasant we're-all-marines-together grin became a frown.

"I'm trying to help a former Secret Service agent who was there on duty that day in November 1963," I said quickly, not giving the sergeant enough time to say anything. "He's literally dying from the guilt of it. What his daughter and I are suggesting is a way to keep him alive. She is waiting outside. Her father lives in Kinderhook—across the river not far from here."

The frown was gone but the smile had not yet returned. Just a hint of curiosity was there.

It was enough to keep me talking. "He was the Secret Service agent who decided to take down the bubble top from the presidential limousine. He believes it was a decision that led to the death of Kennedy. That belief has led to a mental breakdown that has turned physical and brought him to the brink of death."

The sergeant seemed ready to respond. I let him.

"How could that be?" he asked. "I don't get it."

Oh, Sergeant, I thought but did not say, *you are on the route to being had. You just opened the door. Maybe.*

Once I finished going through the various theories and possibilities, Sergeant Lambert asked the only question that mattered. "What exactly do you need from the marines, sir?"

"I need to borrow—or rent—a high-powered rifle as similar as possible to the one Oswald used," I said.

"To do what exactly?"

"Fire into Plexiglas and see what happens."

Lambert reached for the phone and dialed a number. "Gunny, this is Lambert over at recruiting," he said into the receiver. "I've got a former marine who is looking for a particular weapon."

He listened for a few seconds and said, "Thanks, Gunny. His name is . . ." He looked up at me.

"Gilmore. Jack Gilmore," I prompted from across the desk.

"Jack Gilmore," the sergeant repeated. "He was a platoon commander in One-Nine. I'll send him right over."

Lambert hung up and tore a sheet of paper from a memo pad on his desk. He wrote down a name, an address, and some directions then slid the paper across to me.

I took it in one hand, shook the sergeant's vigorously with the other, and said, "Thank you, Sergeant."

"A pleasure, Lieutenant," said the sergeant. "You're in the Ready Reserves, right?"

I nodded.

"Well, I'd bet the corps would put you on active duty in a flash and promote you to captain just like that," the sergeant said, snapping his fingers. "They're needing every officer they can get in 'Nam right now."

"I hear you, Sergeant. Semper Fi."

"Semper Fi, Lieutenant," Lambert said in response.

That's short for *Semper Fidelis*—always faithful. It's how marines say good-bye to one another.

MARTI HAD NO trouble following the directions to Gunny's Weapons and Wisdom, a gun and military surplus shop barely a mile away.

"I think I've found a place to get the Plexiglas," she reported with excitement as we rode.

Marti, with my consultation, was trying to locate six one-quarter-inch-thick pieces that roughly replicated those I had seen myself on the Kennedy limo and in a couple of photographs since. None of the big hardware stores had what we needed, she said. Neither did half a dozen glass repair shops she called. One said they did have a small supply of Plexiglas, but the pieces they described sounded too thin and small.

"But there's a Mack Truck sales, repair, and body shop up north of the city," Marti said. "Based on what they told me on the phone, they not only have the right size and texture Plexiglas, they also have all the saws and stuff it'll take to cut it into pieces the way we want."

I told her that was just great. Good work for a kid college student majoring in American literature.

But first there was the weapon.

"Jonah Dickens (Gunny)" was the name the sergeant had written down on the memo paper. I resisted Marti's push to come inside with me. I had almost given up trying to do or not do anything that did not suit her. She was, well . . . hard to resist. But she did agree to stay in the car.

There were no other customers in Gunny's shop, which was a place unlike any I had seen since I left the Marine Corps. Standing behind a glass display counter of rifles, pistols, and other firearms, Gunny Dickens appeared more normal than I was expecting. He was a clean-shaven, paunchless, shaved-head man in his mid-forties who wore a dark green sweater and freshly starched olive-green dungarees, carefully bloused with rubber bands over the top of spit-shined dark brown combat boots—items from the standard marines' field uniform of the day.

After an introduction and my explanation about who sent me, he and I made some small talk about our respective records. He had been a gunnery sergeant in Korea, where he'd nearly frozen to death at the Chosin Reservoir. He went through a descriptive list of his various body parts and fluids that had been frozen. He spoke in a low, gravelly voice that, like everything else about him, was standard issue.

The chitchat finally finished, I said, "I'm looking for a rifle like the one Oswald used to shoot Kennedy."

"The whole world knows that Oswald never fired a round at Kennedy," Gunny Dickens said without so much as a blink. "They planted that palm print on the stock of the rifle and then hid it behind those boxes at that Texas School Book Depository building to implicate Oswald and then set him up for Ruby to kill him."

I remained silent as Gunny went on.

"The killers of John F. Kennedy on November twenty-second, 1963, were a squad of seven Mafia-trained CIA assassins who were paid by a rich anti-Catholic defrocked Episcopalian priest fanatic with ties to Castro, Johnson, and Steinbrenner, the leadership of South African army intelligence, Merrill Lynch, Chrysler, and the New York Yankees."

I said only, "Mmmmmmm."

He went on. "The Kennedy killing team fired twelve shots—four from up and behind through four different windows in two separate buildings, two below street level on Elm Street directly below from a sewer culvert, three from the grassy knoll up north and on the west side of the motorcade, two from the railroad underpass directly in front, and, of course, one from inside the presidential limousine itself by a rogue Secret Service agent."

Though I had heard this kind of crap many times in my post-assassination reporting, I had never heard it spit out in such a one-two-three organized fashion and with so many details aggregated into one idiotic plot.

I still said nothing but I was careful to maintain eye contact—to at least fake hanging on his every stupid word.

"Why do you want such a weapon?" Gunny finally asked.

"I want to try a reenactment," I said.

"Why? I just told you what happened. Everybody knows it."

"I have a friend with a serious, personal reason to find out what would have happened had there been a bubble top on Kennedy's car when the shots were fired," I said.

Gunny nodded. That's all he did. He just nodded. I knew from my own reporting experiences that conspiracy nuts had conversations like this as routinely as if they were about whether cheeseburgers are better with mustard or mayonnaise.

"The rifle they claim was used on Kennedy, of course, was an Italian Carcano bolt-action, single-shot 6.5-caliber piece of nineteen-ninety-five mail-order junk," Gunny said. "There's no way in hell it could have hit both Kennedy and Connally—" He stopped himself from going on.

"I don't have one of those," Gunny continued after a beat. "But I've got something as close as you can get. It's a Model 39 Mosin-Nagant sport rifle made in Finland about the same time as the alleged assassination Italian piece."

He motioned for me to follow him and, after unlocking three doors, one of them of solid steel, we went into a back room that contained enough weaponry to outfit a small army. There were dozens of pistols, automatic rifles, grenades, and rocket launchers, along with a couple of sixty-millimeter mortars and even a flamethrower.

After looking about the vault for a few minutes, Gunny handed me a bolt-action rifle with a telescopic sight that very much resembled the weapon Oswald—or whoever—used to kill John F. Kennedy. Both the dark brown wood stock and the metal parts glistened from polish and care. Gunny told me that rifles like this were mostly used by snipers in Russia and Eastern Europe.

"Here's a box of seven rounds," he said. "Don't be wasteful—there's not much of this kind of stuff."

I promised to use the ammo wisely.

And when I asked what it was all going to cost to rent it for a couple of days, Gunny said: "The ammo's a dollar a round. I gave you the four extra in case you wanted to practice a bit first. The rifle's yours to use—on the house, marine to marine. Pay for the ammo when you return the weapon. Just clean it before you bring it back, Lieutenant."

I said I would do that. That was a rule of the shooting road. No professional ever returns a borrowed weapon uncleaned. Gunny handed me a cleaning kit, which was a fold-up rod with cloth swabs that were thrust up and down inside the barrel of the rifle after firing. I'd had plenty of experience doing that to the M1 rifle I used during my officers' and infantry training.

"Some people think that Kennedy would have lived, no matter what, if they'd kept the bubble top on the Kennedy limo," I said as we parted, just to give Gunny one last turn-on. "Might have deflected the shots or scared off Oswald to begin with."

"Only some weirdo on dope would ever believe a thing like that," Gunny said. "Oswald never knew that Carcano rifle existed till the cops found it after the assassination behind those boxes where the CIA's mob hit team planted it."

Gunny, like all good marines, seldom disappointed—even when talking absolute nonsense.

As I WALKED out of Gunny's carrying that rifle, I knew that for at least this exact moment in time, Marti Walters adored me. A worshipful look flashed across her face that was unlike anything I had ever seen.

She grabbed me long and hard when I finally sat down by her in the right front passenger seat of the Pontiac wagon after carefully laying the rifle on the floor of the backseat.

"You really are wonderful, Jack," she said. "I will sing the 'Marines' Hymn' in your honor for the rest of my life."

I thought she might add a few tears of joy to her demonstration of appreciation but she held back.

We still had another important stop to make.

She drove us nearly forty-five minutes north to the Mack Truck shop. It took only a few minutes for two men in the parts department to pull out two large sheets of Plexiglas and then, per my instructions, cut them into the six pieces that we were going to need.

I stacked them carefully in the backseat as Marti handed a ten-dollar bill to the guy in charge. I didn't know the going rate for Plexiglas but that seemed awfully cheap to me. Maybe he had been charmed by Marti. Whatever happened, we drove off from the truck place.

"So, what now?" I said.

Our planning had been undertaken with what could only be termed a one-step-at-a-time approach. I had more or less insisted on that, because I was really doubtful we would ever get our hands on a suitable rifle, among the other necessary things. Frankly, I was mostly just playing along. I never thought we would get this far in staging the reenactment Marti had in mind.

"We go back to Kinderhook—and then to Lindenwald," Marti said, her face in a huge grin.

"Lindenwald?"

"Martin Van Buren's old house. The tower would be perfect. I think it would have a special meaning to Dad for it to be there, too."

"For what to be there?"

"Our reenactment—of course."

We rode in silence for a few minutes, long enough for an obvious thought to finally find a logical place in my mind.

"You know, Marti," I said, "we don't have to go to all of that big reenactment trouble to find out what your dad needs to find out."

She didn't even turn her head in my direction. "I *know* that," she said.

Just to make sure we were talking about the same thing, I said: "We could go into a secluded place in some woods, put up a piece of the Plexiglas somewhere, and take a shot at it from ninety feet away at the appropriate angle . . ."

"Don't even suggest such a thing."

"Why not? Then we'd know now—right now, without having to produce some crazy staged shooting from a tower. We'd know. And we could just tell him. We could save him from all this effort."

"Tell him we already know what's going to happen when those shots are fired?"

"No, no. Maybe we don't tell him anything. But if it doesn't shatter we could keep quiet and try to think of something else or turn it over to Reynolds to do his thing . . ."

"Don't tell Dad if it turns out that the glass does not shatter? Tell him only if it does?"

Her question had no answer. She wasn't really listening to me. Clearly, there *had* to be a reenactment, and that was that.

Glancing harshly at me, she said, "It has to be an honest reenactment for it to work for Dad. He would know if it were not real—not straight. He would know if we already knew what was going to happen. Dr. Reynolds wouldn't approve of that, either. He believes in *real* reliving therapy."

I very much doubted the veracity of either of her points but I chose not to answer, letting the silence take over the last several minutes of our drive back to Kinderhook.

I also doubted that she adored me quite as much as she had a few minutes ago.

OVER THE NEXT two days, I came to believe Marti Walters was the smartest, toughest twenty-year-old kid, male or female, I had ever encountered—marines included.

She brought an energetic sharpness to every aspect of the

planning and preparation of our Lindenwald adventure. She also had an abundance of shout, guile, and charm, with the sense to know when and in what proportions to employ each.

"Dad, always remember that this is about you and for you," she said to Van Walters when we first told him what her "team"—she and I plus maybe her mother—were planning.

He kept his eyes open and his head up as we began going through the details. But he started shaking his head maybe fifteen minutes in, as I was explaining how I was going to arrange the six pieces of Plexiglas into a makeshift version of the bubble top.

"What is it?" Marti asked her father.

"Never going to work, never going to work, never going to work."

"I've got some strong masking tape to keep the pieces together," I said quickly in response.

"Never going to work, never going to work, never going to work."

Van Walters closed his eyes and leaned his head back against the pillow on the chaise lounge where he still spent most of his days and nights.

Marti stuck her face right down in his and shouted: "You listen to me, Special Agent Walters! You listen to me with every ounce of whatever you have left in your mind and soul!"

His eyes popped open.

"You are dying! D-y-i-n-g—dying! The only thing that can save your life is if Jack and I can prove something to you that will convince you that you do not have to die!"

No Parris Island DI could have matched the force with which that little American literature major delivered those words.

"Kennedy would have died no matter what you did about that bubble top! No matter what! That is the fact and we are going to prove it to you! Let's go get our work done, Jack!"

My marine instincts almost had me saluting and saying, *Aye, aye, ma'am!* despite my own very real question about what would happen once those shots were fired. I had no idea—and neither, of course, did Marti—if the glass was going to shatter or deflect, if it was going to protect or kill.

Out in the hallway with the door slammed by Marti behind us, she said in her normal voice, "I'm going to have to shake him and shake him. Keep on him and stay on him. But right now let's go check the tower to make sure it works."

I followed without a word.

Marti had used a Walters family connection to convince the owners of Lindenwald and the Kinderhook police that there were good reasons for allowing the live firing of three rifle shots down at some Plexiglas ninety feet on the ground below. "It's part of a very confidential exercise—that I don't fully understand the extent of myself—to explore several unknowns about presidential assassinations." That was the line she used.

I was not with her for that conversation, so all I know is what she told me. "I sealed the deal when I told them that a marine sharpshooter who'd won the Medal of Honor in Korea and had investigated the Kennedy assassination for a government commission was going to do the actual shooting." Guile, guile—lots of guile. Lies, lies—lots of lies.

The federal government had recently begun a process for eventually taking over ownership as well as possession of Lindenwald, the eighth president's house. The plan was eventually to restore the three-story mansion to its early splendor and to open it to the public. The critical word was *eventually*. For now it remained vacant in a well-worn, deteriorating state having been used, at various times, as a privately owned residence and a for-rent venue for parties.

We drove off Highway 9 down a short gravel road. When the house came into view, we followed a drive and stopped behind the building.

Marti had been given a key to the place by a member of the family that owned Lindenwald. We used it to enter through a back door on the first floor and took a staircase that we knew led up to the tower, which rose another floor higher above the house itself. The place was a mess of cracked plaster walls and ceilings, warped and scarred wooden doors. There were small stacks of junk around—hardened paintbrushes, dead potted plants, scraps of carpet, old newspapers and magazines. The staircase, large and square-cornered, was enclosed by plaster walls adorned by a few cheap paintings and sketches of nineteenth-century gentry and scenery. The stairs and banisters were a dark brown wood that was badly in need of refinishing and varnish. We kicked up whiffs of must and dust with each step we took.

I figured the preservation feds were going to arrive here in barely the nick of time to save Lindenwald from its aging and neglect.

But the inside of Lindenwald was not what Marti's and my excursion was about. What mattered was the view from the tower's ten-foot-by-ten-foot-square portico. It was covered with an Italianate roof but open on all four sides.

Within a few seconds, I knew this was going to work for our enactment.

I had stood and knelt at the sixth-floor window of the Texas School Book Depository more than a dozen times while working on various stories for the *Tribune*. I was always struck by how close everything was. Ninety feet from the window down to where the presidential limousine was moving at barely fifteen miles an hour seemed like it was close enough to touch the Kennedys and the Connallys. Like many others who had also been to the window, I was not surprised that Oswald hit his target. It would have been an easy shot for almost anyone with any level of marksmanship training. Oswald, who was a former marine—a fact that pained me every time I had to write it in my newspaper—would have definitely had that training.

I felt exactly the same way about the vantage point now, looking down from the Lindenwald tower portico. The angles and distance were nearly identical. There were even some light tree branches in both lines of sight. It was spooky.

"You were right, it really is perfect," I said to Marti.

She threw her arms around me and held on tight. "Thank you, Jack," she said. "Let's go shake Dad some more."

———

MY NEW REPORT to Van Walters had his attention from the beginning. I couldn't tell if it was sinking in, but there was a new, brighter light in his eyes. A light of life? Of interest? I couldn't tell.

"The same angle and distance?" he said to me.

"Yes, sir," I said. "Almost exactly."

He said: "I know Lindenwald from back when I was a kid. I played up there in the tower . . . threw rocks, shot BB guns down from there at birds and squirrels. Wasn't supposed to, of course, but we did it. Got caught a few times but nothing came of it. The Secret Service would have never hired me if I had a juvenile record. Did Marti ever tell you about Martin Van Buren Bates?"

I shook my head and said, "No, sir."

Marti rolled her eyes and said quickly: "Dad told me about him. He was the tallest man in the world—seven feet eleven inches tall, married a woman seven feet. They met in a freak show while on tour in England. Love at giant sight. Now let's get on to the business at hand . . ."

But I had question. And out of simple curiosity, I asked: "Why did his parents name him Martin Van Buren? Was he from Kinderhook?"

Van Walters laughed—for the first time ever in my presence—and answered: "No, Kentucky. Van Buren was president when their son was born so they named their own big man for the biggest man of the day."

That was enough of that for Marti. "Let's forget the freaks

now, Dad. Jack says the view downward from the Lindenwald tower really is a perfect match for Dallas," she said sternly, underlining my earlier point, and then adding a very important new one. "You'll be able to see that for yourself, of course."

The light in Van Walters dimmed slightly.

"You're coming to Lindenwald, Dad, with us—that's the plan and that is what you will do," said his daughter.

"I don't know about that," he mumbled.

"Yes, you do. I just told you."

The next step in the Marti-directed show-and-tell was the rifle that would be used. She motioned to me.

"Take a look at this," I said, holding the Finnish sport rifle across my chest with both hands. "You want to hold it, sir?"

Walters tossed his head to the side. *No thank you, reporter/friend, whoever you are.* But he did give the rifle a steady look from the tip of the barrel down through the sight and bolt to the wooden stock.

"Some weapon," said Walters.

"Almost identical to the one Oswald used, sir," I said.

"How do you know that?" Walters said. There was a snap to it. Maybe all of this was, in fact, getting to him.

"A marine firearms expert told me, sir."

Van Walters moved his body straight forward as if he was going to stand up. "What is your time line, Marti, for this reenactment of yours?" he asked, turning directly to his daughter.

"Two days from today, Dad—Tuesday morning," she said.

She was about to burst with energy and something close to pleasure.

"It's going to be cold out there, isn't it?" Van Walters said.

"Yes, but we'll bundle you up well."

That annoyed him. "I was thinking about the shooting, not my physical comfort," he snapped. "Cold weather can affect the accuracy of a bullet's trajectory."

Another sign of real life from this man!

"I must do some walking over the next two days . . . and maybe even outside . . . to get myself ready," he said, as if he was talking to himself.

Then to me: "Those fools at the Warren Commission should have done a reenactment on that bubble top. They would've seen what difference it would have made. God knows the FBI idiots wouldn't have done such a thing. All they were interested in was protecting themselves. You know, the FBI knew Oswald was in Dallas but they never told us. He wasn't on any threat list. If we had known he was there and was a commie defector with marine rifle training now working at the book depository building, we'd have gotten him out of there—put him in some kind of protective custody or done something ahead of time. There'd never have been an assassination. Kennedy would still be alive right now, maybe serving a second term. I so wish he were still alive. I hate it that we let him die. I hate it that I let him die."

Former Secret Service special agent Martin Van Walters stood up under his own power and wandered out of the room.

Afterward, amid flowing tears of absolute joy, his daughter

said to me: "He has not talked that much like that since . . . since I don't know how long ago. I need to tell Mom."

I went with her to give the good news to Rosemary, who was in a small sewing room on the other side of the house. She was reading a copy of *McCall's* magazine. The smell of alcohol was everywhere.

Marti told her what her dad had just done—and said.

"Great," she said, in a slight slur. "But if those bullets don't do the right thing when they hit that glass, won't it only make it worse for him?"

Marti frowned and angrily motioned for me to join her in getting the hell out of there.

Outside, I made no comment on the truth that Rosemary Walters, drunk or not, had just uttered. Neither did Marti.

That remained the unspoken cloud over all that we were doing and what was to come on Tuesday morning.

8

The good news was that the weather forecast called for a high in the mid-forties the day we chose for the reenactment. At this time of year, that was considered a heat wave by the locals of Kinderhook. Also, the sky was clear and sunny with no rain or any other weather on the horizon for the day—a monumental day for a former Secret Service agent and his family, no matter the result.

There were monumental possibilities for me, too, frankly. Confused feelings of guilt and anxiety were rising with the passing of every second, the speaking of every word.

I had been on the phone twice with Bernie Shapiro since my arrival at Kinderhook. "Okay, whattya got?" That's how he started both of our conversations, as he did with almost every *Tribune* reporter, no matter his or her location or story. I often wondered if he said that when his wife or kids called: *Whattya got, sweetheart? Whattya got, Bernie Junior?*

"It's coming together," I said to Bernie, more or less, both times.

"A little more specific, please, Young Jack," he answered, more or less, both times.

"Can't talk now, Bernie. Sorry."

"We on the record yet?" he asked.

"Not quite."

"What does that mean?"

Both times I ended the conversation with a phony excuse that someone was coming into the room where the telephone was. I had to dispense with my burning desire to follow up on his earlier talk about a possible new assignment that would require a passport. One thing—story, assignment—at a time. I was very busy right now.

Since arriving, I had, of course, taken complete notes on everything that had been said and done in Kinderhook by everybody. They were rapidly filling up my reporter's spiral notebook, which I hid between the mattress and box spring of the bed after each nightly writing session in my freezing third-floor room. Marti had not made a second late-night visit here. I didn't expect her to. But I didn't want to take any chance of the notebook's being found.

The anxiety was coming with the knowledge that my moment of truth—literally—was fast approaching. Was I a hungry, ambitious reporter about to figure out a way to violate (or ignore) a confidence in order to break a big story? Or was I a wonderful, selfless new friend who arrived, like Superman, to rescue the lives and happiness of a sick man and his desperate young daughter?

I was certain I would have to answer the question no matter what the three rounds I fired from the Finnish sniper rifle did to the Plexiglas. The glass shatters. A probable step toward a dramatic cure for former agent Walters? The glass deflects the bullets. Agent Walters either remains down and sick or begins to get even worse? Either way, a good story for *The Dallas Tribune* and all ships at sea. Or, no story at all because of the off-the-record deal?

Marti and I had no choice but to include Rosemary Walters in the operation, because we realized that we might need some additional help getting our show on—and off—the road. One of the reasons for staging the event in the morning was to mitigate the certainty that Marti's mother would come to the task lubricated with alcohol. Managing how much she could consume by nine o'clock in the morning was a lot easier than keeping her away from the stuff any longer.

I'd had an unplanned private conversation with Rosemary just before dinner. We happened to run into each other in a small second-floor sitting room off to one side of the house. She was sitting by herself with a glass of something and an *Atlantic* magazine. And she was smoking a cigarette. So be it. It was her turf. *I* wasn't going to do that here.

"You're not really Marti's boyfriend, are you?" she asked without preamble.

"Maybe more of a future possibility than a present reality," I said, not having really thought about what I was saying. Was it a future possibility? Not if I broke the off-the-record agreement.

"One thing you should know," she said, her magazine now in her lap, her glass on the table. I was still standing in front of her. "I seldom drank before November twenty-second, before Van got sick about what he believed he did, before we went to Singapore in search of cures and salvation."

"I understand, Mrs. Walters," I said.

"No, I don't think you do. You think I'm a worthless drunk who has left my husband and daughter for the bottle."

"No, ma'am. I do not think that . . ."

"I'm a ricochet in this little family drama, Jack. That's what I am. The shrapnel hit Van front and center and then glanced off and came right at me. Thank God, we—*I*—had sense enough to get Marti out of the line of fire or she'd probably have taken even worse hits than she has."

"I hear you loud and clear, ma'am. I really do understand what you're saying."

As I moved away, I did everything I could to memorize exactly what Rosemary Walters had just said. That "ricochet" quote cried out to have a prominent place in what I would eventually write.

THINGS DID NOT start well the next morning. In fact, we almost lost control of the whole thing before it really began.

"I am not going," Van Walters announced at eight fifteen. He was once again slouched in the sitting room chaise, having made no effort to dress for the mission ahead. He was still wearing a dark brown robe over wrinkled pajamas. "This is not going to work. I just know this is not going to work."

We had assembled downstairs in Van's room to begin our final preparations. Marti had warned us that something like this might happen despite all the good signs since we'd laid out our plan. He said this to Marti and me and her mother, who, joy of joys, gave off not even a whiff of a drink.

Her father, over the last two days, had in fact become slightly stronger physically. He had increased the size and number of meals he ate and took two "practice" walks outside accompanied once by Marti, the other time by Rosemary. But Marti reminded me repeatedly that her dad was still a very sick man and it was unrealistic to think he was going to suddenly get better. Even if the Plexiglas did shatter, it would at best be only the beginning of his very long recovery, not the ending. Dr. Reynolds, with whom Marti had stayed in steady contact by phone, agreed.

Now, after her father's balking statements, Marti calmly signaled me with a head motion. Without a word, I dutifully followed her to the front door of the house and waved to the car outside.

It was Reynolds—our safety valve. He had agreed to be present for our reenactment but only to observe and stand by in case of an emergency. He had driven over from Boston last night and stayed in a motel near Kinderhook.

I met Reynolds between the car and the house and, as we walked, told him the latest setback with Van Walters.

And Walters said to Reynolds immediately when they saw each other a few moments later, "This is not going to work, Reynolds. Forget it."

"It already *is* working, Mr. Walters," Reynolds said smoothly.

"What do you mean?" Walters barked back. I couldn't help noticing how much his voice was beginning to sound like his daughter's.

"Listen to yourself, look at yourself—you are a different man from the one I saw and talked to a few days ago," said Reynolds. "You're already on the way toward being alive again."

Walters lifted his head but nothing more of himself. "No matter what happens to that Plexiglas, nothing is going to be resolved," he said.

"Why not?" Reynolds asked, still speaking soothingly. "I don't understand."

Walters looked away.

After a few seconds, Reynolds said, "If I may open up a difficult possibility for you, Mr. Walters. Let's say Jack fires his three shots, as planned, and the bullets ricochet off the glass."

The face of Van Walters turned to that of a boy about to face an angry school principal. "That would prove it!"

"Prove what, exactly?"

"That I was responsible for the death of Kennedy and we'd be right back where this all started," Walters said, pointing a finger against the side of his head. I read that to mean that he would be crazy—again? Still?

"What if the glass splits up into many sharp and dangerous pieces that become flying weapons?"

Walters stood up. "All right, all right. Let me get dressed."

Good work, Dr. Safety Valve!

Van Walters walked into a small adjoining room that he had been using as a bedroom and dressing room and closed the door behind him.

Marti and I exchanged right thumbs-up with each other—and then Reynolds. Rosemary Walters just smiled. I had the feeling that she had taken a tranquilizer of some kind. One of an odorless sort, at least.

MARTI DIRECTED THE seating assignments for the station wagon. She drove, her mother rode in the passenger seat, and I sat in the back with her father. Reynolds followed in his own car.

All of us were dressed properly for forty-degree coolness—sweaters under jackets with gloves and caps. Van Walters needed no special orders. He wore heavy, baggy dark green corduroy pants, a heavy black wool jacket over at least two layers of shirts, bulky gloves, and his brown felt Secret Service snap-brimmed hat. Nobody had to hold an arm or help him in or out of the car.

After parking behind Lindenwald, Marti told her father and mother to remain in the station wagon, which both did without comment or protest. There was no doubt about Marti being in charge. She left the motor running with the heater on.

Marti and I began putting everything in its proper place for the reenactment. We had carefully loaded and arranged all of the equipment in the large rear storage compartment of the Pontiac Safari so each item could be brought out in the order needed.

First, we assembled the card tables. There were four of them, two we borrowed from neighbors "for a party." We carried them to a spot on the ground below the tower we had identified as being roughly one hundred feet from where the shots would be fired. Then we brought out the six pieces of Plexiglas and, using the masking tape, set the panels together on the tables the way we planned. The end result had the look of a clear plastic rectangular box that was four feet high and just over six feet long. My measurements of the glass panels had been eyeballed estimates, but this result was a remarkably consistent replica of the bubble top that had been taken off the back of the presidential limousine that fateful afternoon. I worked from my memory but also from some photographs I had found in various newspaper and magazine articles at the Kinderhook public library.

Our assembly took barely five minutes. Marti and I had rehearsed this a couple of times yesterday in the secluded backyard of the family house.

Next came three small canvas folding chairs. We set them on the ground roughly halfway between the tower and the card tables but several yards away from what was soon to be the line of fire. These were for the audience on the sidelines—the critical eyewitness chairs.

Marti went to the Pontiac, leaned in and turned off the ignition, and said to her parents, "Come with me. We're almost ready."

Van Walters was pointed to sit in the middle chair with Marti on his left, Rosemary on his right. The view of the bubble top was unobstructed for all three. Whatever the three rounds I fired did to that Plexiglas had to be clearly observable. I had been slightly concerned that deflected pieces of bullets or splintered glass—whatever the case would be—might fly toward the Walterses. I was most mindful of Rosemary's talk of her being a kind of ricochet victim. I sure as hell didn't want her daughter or husband to be a literal one. But I determined, mostly by uncalculated speculation, that both the distances and the likely lines of flight presented no serious hazard. And Marti barely listened to me when I laid out the possibilities of danger.

The show must go on!

Now Marti went to the house and unlocked the back door. Curtain time was approaching.

She went to sit with her father and mother while I removed the rifle from the rear of the station wagon's back storage space. I had wrapped it in a gray wool blanket.

I noticed Reynolds, now out of his car, taking a position behind some trees so he could watch the shots hit the glass but also witness Van's reactions. He had assured Marti that he was prepared to step into the picture, whatever it might look like, if and when it seemed necessary to do so.

I slammed the car trunk and held the rifle with both hands across my chest with the barrel raised to my left at a level just above my head and the butt down below the waist—at port, as they said in the military. I approached the back door and began my trip up the winding staircase.

My head was jumping with complicated, confusing, contradictory thoughts. I knew that I would do the shooting the way it needed to be done. I had known for years how to handle rifles—even before I was in the marines—because of my dad. He took me hunting for coyotes, groundhogs, and rabbits. We even went skeet shooting several times with rifles equipped with scope sights, which he taught me how to adjust. So even without a test firing of the Finnish weapon, I was sure the shooting would be no problem.

Carrying the rifle brought back being a marine. Sergeant Lambert. His Silver Star. Vietnam. His Purple Heart. And I was hit by a powerful thought: *I'm not there. I am in Kinderhook, New York, shooting at Plexiglas. Real Marines are in Vietnam being shot* at. I thought about Rosemary Walters, that poor woman who was there but not ever really there. The other Walters family casualty. Marti Walters. She was just a kid. What were my feelings about her? They were all over the place.

Is the Plexiglas going to shatter all over the place? What if it doesn't? Van Walters goes into a further funk and dies? Isn't it a better story for me if he does *die? What an outrageous thought! My story. How do I convince Marti to let me write and report her father's story? How do I either pass through or work around off-the-record? Lovely Marti. Tough Marti. Smart Marti. How in the hell am I going to manage her?*

I arrived at the top of the tower, stepped up through the opening to the floor of the portico. I went to the closed waist-high wooden railing that faced the south side of the grounds, where the Plexiglas was mounted on the card tables on the ground below.

I carefully put the rifle on the top of the railing, using the blanket as a surface to rest the gun. I wanted to make damn sure I got no scratches on Gunny Dickens's valuable weapon.

I knelt down to the firing position. My left hand cradled the front part of the rifle as I gently settled the butt into my right shoulder and brought my right arm and hand forward across the stock to the trigger.

I leaned forward and put my right eye on the telescopic sight. I was confident I could properly adjust the sight to hit the target. I went through the process meticulously. I found the Plexiglas in the crosshairs. Moved the small adjustment wheel to heighten the image. Then I moved the rifle away from the target to a leaf on a nearby tree to test the sighting before returning to the glass box.

I was ready.

"Ready if you are!" I shouted down at the Walterses.

Marti looked up at the open tower, me, and my rifle. "Ready, Jack," she hollered back.

I pulled open the rifle bolt, removed a long shiny brass-jacketed bullet from a pocket, shoved it in the chamber, pushed the bolt forward, and locked it down.

I switched off the safety.

"First shot!" I yelled.

I put the sight with the crosshairs on the bubble top just above the front panel, aiming for a spot at the top of the glass.

I took a deep breath, slowly squeezed the trigger.

Pow!

The rifle kicked back against my shoulder—just as I had remembered it would.

I could see that the bullet hit the glass and ricocheted forward, leaving the glass undamaged.

Ricocheted forward leaving the glass undamaged!

I yanked the bolt open, and the empty shell casing flew to the floor. I inserted another bullet.

"Second shot!" I yelled.

I sighted a place in the back glass panel about where the head of a person sitting in the backseat of the limo would be.

I squeezed the trigger.

There was another simultaneous *Pow!* and kick.

I saw the bullet hit the Plexiglas in the center—right where I had aimed. It seemed from my view that it made a hole and then flew off to the left. But it was hard to tell for sure.

One more to go.

"Third shot!"

This time, again just as I had intended, the bullet struck the side panel on the right. I saw some cracking of the glass, and then the bullet slug seemed to tail off forward to the right. Another ricochet?

I quickly grabbed the three expended bullet casings off the floor and, with the rifle and the blanket, raced down the stairwell as fast as I could.

I went from the bottom floor in one leap out the door to the ground, and then around to the south side where Marti and her family had been seated.

The first things I saw were the unmoving bodies and heads of Marti, Van, and Rosemary Walters. They sat in those three folding chairs like three statues. They seemed paralyzed. Stunned. Frozen.

I went up behind them. "Let's go see exactly what happened to the glass," I said.

Nobody said a word or even looked back at me.

Finally, Van Walters stood. He took a deep breath that, from his back, seemed to have begun down in his toes and come out through the top of his felt hat. It was as if he were a large rubber balloon that had been inflated and then immediately deflated.

Van Walters began walking toward our card table assembly. I moved around to his side. Marti and Rosemary followed us. Not a word had yet been spoken except by me.

"Let's look at them one shot at a time," I said to Van Walters.

Walters nodded. All four of us moved to the bubble top.

Shot one. There was a heavy, deep scratch on the top panel, obviously where the bullet had hit and been deflected.

Shot two. A bullet hole in the back panel. There was some small cracking surrounding the hole. Where had the bullet gone from there? I led the three Walterses around to the left side. There was another hole there. It was smaller, clearly an exit hole. The bullet, in other words, had gone through the panel, slowed down and thrown off its direct path to the left, where it made another hole and disappeared somewhere out there in the Lindenwald lawn.

Shot three. There was a long, severe perforation on the

right panel with much more cracking than in either of the first two shots. But the bullet, again, kept moving off into the countryside somewhere.

"I'll go see if I can find the three slugs," I said, a statement that drew no answer.

And there we stood, the four of us in what had become a rough circle. Van, Rosemary, and Marti Walters—and me, Jack Gilmore, reporter-adorer-helper-marksman-liar/honest-man? ("Still to kum," as they write at the end of a piece of unfinished newspaper copy.)

I kept my eyes on Marti, who had hers focused on her father. I could tell something was about to give.

"Oh, Daddy, oh, Daddy," Marti sobbed, throwing her arms around Van Walters. "I had so hoped—believed with all my heart and soul—that Jack's and my six panes of Plexiglas were going to be at least fifty pieces of shattered glass. We would all be yelling *Hip, hip hooray!* The glass pieces would range from ragged hunks to spear-like pointed shards."

"Yes," Rosemary said, putting an arm each around the backs of her husband and daughter and holding tight. "Spear-like pointed shards."

"I was right, I was right," Van Walters said. His voice was sad—but firm. I had begun to expect that right about now something dramatic and awful was going to happen. I had no idea what it might be, but standing only a couple feet away from the Walterses I was at the ready. I had wrapped the blanket back around the rifle and put it on the ground so I had both hands ready to do whatever needed to be done.

"But, Daddy, it doesn't really mean anything," Marti said quickly. "Don't say what you've been saying—thinking—for five years. It doesn't mean that . . ."

"That I killed Kennedy?"

Taller than both his daughter and wife, Van Walters placed his hands on the top of each of their heads.

I tensed up my arms and hands. And I looked back to the trees. Reynolds had moved up to within a few feet of where we were. He, too, was at the ready.

Van Walters said, his voice gaining in strength: "They'd all have been killed. The Kennedys, the Connallys, the agents in the car. If that bubble top had been on the limo they'd all have died." He paused to kiss both women on their foreheads. "That's what all the others said to me over and over. Akins said it. The other agents said it. The doctors said it. You two said it. Everyone said it. But they were all wrong. I was right. The bubble top would have saved Kennedy's life. *I* would have saved Kennedy's life."

"Daddy, you said it right the first time. The bubble top might have saved his life. An inanimate object. Not a person— not you or anyone else. Lee Harvey Oswald, or whoever fired the shots, killed Kennedy. He took life and death upon himself. You didn't . . ."

"Let me see that rifle," Van Walters said to me. It was an order.

So here we were, having arrived at that awful moment I had felt coming.

"I can't do that, sir," I said.

"Give me the rifle, young man!"

I looked over at Marti. *Help!*

Marti, to my horror and surprise, nodded to me. The nod said, *It's okay. Give him the rifle. Give my crazy daddy the rifle.*

I glanced over at Rosemary. She just closed her eyes.

I felt the presence of Reynolds behind me. But he didn't touch me or say anything to me.

"It's not loaded, sir, if you're thinking about doing any-thing . . . you know, rash," I mumbled to Walters.

"Give me some rounds with the weapon." Van Walters had risen to an occasion—an occasion that, I believed without a doubt, was going to lead to somebody getting seriously hurt. If not Van Walters himself, somebody he loved. The only other possible targets were Reynolds and me. He'd have no reason to take either of us out. But . . . this was a mentally disturbed man demanding that I give him ammo to put in a high-powered rifle and his family seemed to think it was just fine.

I looked back at Reynolds. "Do it," the doctor whispered to me. "Give him the rifle—and the bullets."

That left me as the only sane person present. The only per-son who knew that tragedy could be just seconds away.

But I did it. I took the rifle out of the blanket and gave it to Walters along with the four shiny bullets—the spares Gunny had given me.

I felt like a fool. An idiot.

"Relax . . . what is your name again?" Van Walters said to me.

"Jack!" Marti said sternly—almost angrily—to her father. "Jack Gilmore. He's a wonderful man who has gone way, way beyond all limits to help me help you, Daddy. He deserves your respect—as well as your gratitude. We all do."

Marti moved over to me and took my hand.

"Sorry," Van Walters said to me. "I have been in another world."

Then, without a word, Van Walters methodically loaded a round in the Finnish sniper rifle, sighted it at the bubble top, now only six feet away, and fired. The bullet hit the side panel broadside and crashed a large hole in it. He repeated it a second time, making a hole roughly the same size a foot to the right. Then a third another foot off and, finally, the fourth.

There were now four big holes in the Plexiglas evenly arranged, with cracks in the glass coming out of each, but the structure—our simple homemade bubble top that Marti and I put together with tape—was still standing.

"Thank you, Jack," Van Walters said, handing the rifle back to me. "Need any help cleaning it?"

I had been pretty much holding my breath since I'd handed the weapon to Van Walters. It took a few seconds for me to let it go. "No thank you, sir. I'll get it."

By then all of the Walterses were crying and holding on to one another.

I KNEW MARTI would come to my room that night. At the end of our monumental day and evening, she had said softly out of everyone else's hearing, "How about I see you later?"

My smile was the answer. It was automatic. And in the hour or so since her invitation, I had been in a state of panic. What would I say and do? What would she say and do?

How in the world was this all going to end?

Van Walters had not suddenly gone back to being a fully functioning human being. He did not immediately chow down a cheeseburger with french fries, a double-layer chocolate cake, and a Bud, run ten laps around the town of Kinderhook, or have a meaningful discussion about the new anti-Johnson opinion piece (by a former Kennedy administration official) in *Harper's* on how differently Kennedy would have handled Vietnam. (Kennedy would have either not escalated or pulled out altogether.)

"But he's just at the beginning, don't you think?" Marti had said. And even Van himself had said, "I think I can pull out of this. I really do think so now." Those were his exact words.

More important, Dr. Reynolds had said the same thing to Marti. I had always assumed that psychiatrists were more hands-on—couches-on, at least—than Reynolds seemed to be throughout our reenactment adventure. It was something I might try to talk to him about—particularly if and when I wrote my *Tribune* story. Or maybe not.

"But Reynolds also said it was going to take many months to bring Dad back to health physically as well as psychologically," Marti added. "He emphasized that relapses should be anticipated, if not counted on."

I asked her how Reynolds explained what had happened—

why did the result of our reenactment—the opposite of what we wanted—have such a positive effect?

"It is impossible to explain in exact terms," she said Reynolds told her. "He said his best theory is simply that when the glass didn't splinter, it snapped Daddy back into a sense of reality. Firing those four shots on his own was what finally did it. Why, exactly, Reynolds couldn't say. It just happened."

Marti shrugged and smiled. So did I.

We had cleaned up the Plexiglas and other residue from our event and returned the card tables to neighbors and the key to the Lindenwald owners. I found only one of the expended slugs from the rifle. It was embedded in a tree more than a hundred feet away. I figured there was nothing more to be gained or known from locating the others, including those fired by Van Walters. Where they went was so much less important than that they went somewhere out there. I would use the kit Gunny gave me to clean the Finnish sniper rifle and return it to him in the morning on the way to the Albany airport.

I would leave in the morning. Back to Washington. To the Washington bureau of *The Dallas Tribune*. To work. To where Marti was not.

Those thoughts were at the heart of my heart. They were also foremost in my mind, maybe even obscuring my entire future at the moment. Okay, that sounds overly dramatic, but that was how I was feeling as I lay in bed listening to her footsteps approach the door to my little icebox room.

She came in, as before, with a heavy robe over her pajamas.

But this time, in addition to her furry slippers, she also had a big wool shawl around her shoulders and large mittens on her hands.

"I don't have to crawl in bed with you, Jack, to stay warm," she said, sitting down on the large overstuffed pillow that was the closest thing to a chair there was in the room.

She went on, "Thank you so much, Jack. You are my hero for life. Somebody should give you the Medal of Honor. I really mean that."

I could feel my face warming, though I hoped that it didn't show. "I'm just glad I could be of help."

"Mom is going to benefit from all this, too, I think," Marti said. "Reynolds told us he would find her an alcoholism treatment regimen of some kind." She really looked relieved. "I finally asked her that big November twenty-second question of mine, by the way."

I couldn't remember what question she was talking about.

Marti reminded me. "Remember, I wanted to know who she was with when she went to have a drink that first time. She said she sat in the corner of a bar by herself—nobody was with her. I believe her."

That all made me happy. I had grown most sorry for Marti's mother. And most sympathetic.

"But that, too, will take some time," Marti added.

I had lifted myself onto one elbow to talk with her. But small-talk time had ended. The next move was mine. I knew it and I knew Marti knew it.

So. "Let's talk about there being a story about your dad," I said, trying to keep my voice steady, easy. I kept eye contact. "As you know, what has happened makes for a terrific story . . ."

"Not as terrific as if he had died, though. Right?" Her voice had gone as cold as the room.

I had to look away. I could not help myself. She was right about that but I wasn't about to confirm it, of course. "He didn't die," I said. "And because of what you did, he won't die. What you and I did is part of the story I want to tell. It's what we call a good-news story."

"We had a deal, Jack. Everything was off the record."

"I know, I know. But the deal included our willingness to talk about it once the story was over."

"It's *not* over."

"I agree it could be a while before your dad is in full recovery. But meanwhile, there's a case to be made that doing a story about his healing process—the beginning of his healing—might be of help to others."

"I'm sorry, Jack. I was not aware that there are other former agents of the United States Secret Service who were driven psychologically and physically near death because they ordered the bubble top taken off the Kennedy limousine."

I took a couple of deep breaths. "I'll bet there are other agents who were involved in the Dallas visit who are suffering under a tremendous amount of guilt," I said, and, as I did so, I remembered something. "How about Clint Hill? You know . . . the agent who leaped from the backup car to the limo?"

"Yes, of course, I remember Clint Hill. Dad knew him. They worked together in Washington on the presidential protection detail. He pushed Mrs. Kennedy back down in the seat with President Kennedy. But what about him?"

"Nothing. Except I wouldn't be surprised if he had nightmares about what happened and what else he might have done that could have saved Kennedy's life."

Marti stood up and glared at me. "I thought you were an honorable man, Jack Gilmore. A marine and all that."

"I am—at least part of all that. But you also know—knew when we went into this—that I'm a reporter. I am in the story business. This is a terrific story. I very much want to write it for my paper."

I thought she was on the verge of running out the door and slamming it angrily behind her. But she did not move.

"Martin Van Walters is not a story, Jack. He is my father. Even what you call a good-news story—publicity of any kind—about him right now would cause huge humiliation, if not serious harm. It could throw him into a relapse."

"I'm just trying to see . . . well, if you and I could agree to mutually set aside our off-the-record agreement."

"No," she said as if pronouncing the words for a bronzing. "There is no way."

She turned toward the door. Then back to me.

"But I do owe you, Jack."

I froze stock-still.

"Do you want me to get in bed with you?" she asked, as if asking how I wanted my steak cooked.

I defrosted enough to raise a hand from the covers—and shake it in the negative.

"Well, then, the least I can do is drive you to the bus to Albany in the morning," said Marti. "I assume you are still planning to leave tomorrow?"

I nodded.

After she was gone, I went through what I had just missed. The crawl into the bed under the covers next to me, the slow removal of her shawl, then the loosening of her robe . . .

And all the rest.

I MADE AN early-morning call from the Walters family phone for a reservation on an Allegheny Airlines flight to Washington National Airport. Bernie Shapiro and the *Tribune* had provided me an open return ticket when I left six days ago. Six days ago?

I couldn't believe it had been such a short time—for me, at least. Apparently it had not been for Bernie, a fact that I would soon have to deal with—with or without the need of a passport.

Marti and I were coolly civil during the several minutes we spent together—first over coffee and a toasted English muffin in the kitchen and then in the Pontiac station wagon.

"Definitely going to graduate school, right?" I said as we drove the seven blocks to Kinderhook Market, which served as a stop for the Adirondack Trailways bus to Albany.

"Already accepted—even have a graduate assistant's job lined up," she said.

"Congratulations," I said.

"Thank you," she said.

Neither of us said a word about off-the-record or any possible newspaper story. That conversation had started and ended last night.

Marti didn't even get out of the car at the market. We said good-bye and shook hands in the front seat while sitting next to each other. I waved to her after removing my small suitcase and the Finnish sniper rifle, which I had covered up and wrapped tightly with brown paper and tape.

The bus, which came a few minutes later, was only half full, and I took a seat by myself near the front.

I spent the entire hour-long bus ride deep in thought—and deep in unsplendid misery. I knew how to circumvent an off-the-record deal, of course. All of us in the newspaper business did. Get the story from other sources and then double back on the first source. "Might as well release the off-the-record agreement because I have the story anyhow . . ." In this case, I would return immediately to Kinderhook, interview the woman who owned Lindenwald and other people around town who knew about what had been happening to former Secret Service agent Martin Van Walters. I was sure I could locate the cops who would talk about the bubble top incident and our reenactment. I would be a major source myself, of course. I participated in the original event at Love Field and the one at Lindenwald. All that was unreportable would be what Marti had told me. I couldn't be silenced under any umbrella for what *I* saw and said and did. Back in Washington, I would go full dig into the Clint Hill story. What had happened to him and the other agents at Dallas? Any of them transferred the way Van Walters had been? Any of them treated by any doctors for mental problems? Any firings or resignations? Oh, and what about that agent who kept insisting—disturbingly so—that he personally kept the bubble top from ever being put on the Kennedy limo in the first place? Maybe I could find him or a relative who had spoken to him. Once all that was assembled and ready to go to press, I would go to Philadelphia, or wherever she was, show it to Marti, and ask for her comment, if not her cooperation . . .

Jack Gilmore, honorable newspaperman and Semper Fi honest former marine officer, went directly from the bus to a pay phone at the Albany Trailways station and called Bernie—collect.

"No story yet, Bernie, I'm sorry to say," I said, after his "Whattya got, Young Jack?"

"How can that be, for Crissake? You've spent six days and five hundred dollars—at least—for no story? What happened?"

"Don't know yet how it's going to turn out," I said, and then without taking a breath I added, "I stayed in a friend's private home—so there is no hotel room cost, by the way."

"You're not thinking about pulling a Jerry Compton on me, holding this for a book deal sometime down the road, are you?" said Bernie. Compton was the *Tribune* reporter who had taken his Alamo novel/movie money and run. "I know you want to write books when you grow up, too."

"I'd never do anything like that to you, Bernie." That was a lie—kind of. There was nothing I'd rather do than exactly what Jerry Compton did. Write a book, sell it to the movies, write—write, write, and write. And it had already occurred to me, of course, that there could, in fact, be a book someday in the Van and Marti Walters story.

Bernie didn't immediately respond, which I knew usually meant that he either was preparing a blast or had already decided to move on. Hopefully he was ready to move on to my new assignment—whatever it may be. My fingers were crossed.

"Okay, okay, can't win 'em all," said Bernie, to my great, great relief. "As I told you, I've got something else lined up for you anyhow. I'll tell you all about it when you get back this afternoon."

"Tell me now, Bernie. What is it? The White House?"

"No, no, no White House, Young Jack. Vietnam."

"Vietnam!" I had already imagined myself on television questioning Nixon at White House news conferences . . .

"Yeah, Vietnam. Yeah. Things are getting worse—if that's possible. Nobody's quite gotten over the Tet Offensive and the marine withdrawal from Khe Sanh. And of course, the election of Nixon. The campuses are getting wilder. More than half a million U.S. troops there now. The *Tribune* wants to put our own man on the ground. All we're using now is what we get from the wires and The Times News Service. Our guy could do some overall stuff but mostly about Dallas-area troops. You're a natural for the assignment, being a marine. Maybe go for a couple of months."

I told him that sounded fine with me. But it really didn't. And I wasn't sure exactly why.

I got a taxi to take me to Gunny's shop and then on to the airport.

Gunny Dickens, in accordance with the tradition of Semper Fi trust, did not unwrap or otherwise check the weapon to see if I had, in fact, cleaned the barrel and the chamber and the rifle's many other parts. He barely looked at it as I handed it to him.

"How much for the seven rounds, Gunny?" I asked. "I used them all."

"On the house, marine."

"Hey, thanks," I said.

"None of my business, but did you kill something or save something with that rifle, Lieutenant?"

"Saved."

"Learn anything new about the Kennedy shooting?"

"Not a thing."

"I didn't think you would. Semper Fi. Nothing new to learn."

"Semper Fi."

We shook hands, and I returned to the taxi.

I told the driver that I had to make one more stop. The downtown federal building.

SERGEANT LAMBERT'S FRONT desk at the recruiting office was unoccupied, but a voice from the rear called out to me:

"What can I do for you, young man?" The voice had a

taste of Bernie's "Young Jack" to it but I put it aside when I saw a marine officer, a major, coming toward me. I could tell his rank from the gold leaves on his shirt collar.

"I was looking for Sergeant Lambert, sir," I said.

"He's not here. He's out on a call—talking to some kids about to graduate from high school north of town," said the major. He was a tall, thin, late-forties man with a blond crew cut and three rows of ribbons on his chest. One of them was a Silver Star.

"Could you give him a message, please, sir?"

"Certainly," said the major, leaning down on Lambert's desk to grab a pen and a piece of paper.

"My name is Jack Gilmore. I'm a former marine. One-Nine—platoon commander, got out in '62. Sergeant Lambert did me a favor, and the message is—"

"Lambert told me about you," the major interrupted. "He sure did. Said he put you in touch with Gunny Dickens."

"That's right, yes, sir. Please tell the sergeant that everything turned out well. And that I thank him for his help."

"I will do that. With pleasure."

My business with the marines was now finished. And I turned to go.

"You know, Lieutenant, Sergeant Lambert said he put the arm on you about maybe going back on active duty."

I stood absolutely still. "He sure did, sir. Yes, sir, he sure did."

"Hold on a minute while I get something for you out of my office."

I held on for a minute right there where I was standing until the major returned. He had a piece of paper in his hand.

"If you're so inclined, Lieutenant, all you have to do is sign this, turn it in at Headquarters Marine Corps in Washington, and you could be on your way to being a marine again," the major said.

I took the paper in my hand, thanked him, and snapped my fingers as Sergeant Lambert had the other day.

Then I went outside to the airport taxi that would take me to the plane for Washington.

MARTI WROTE ME a note that was dated exactly a year to the day after we parted at the Kinderhook bus stop. But her letter took more than ninety days to make its way from the Washington bureau of *The Dallas Tribune,* where she assumed I still worked, to Vietnam, where, as a captain, I was commander of Bravo Company, Third Battalion, Third Marines.

She said her father continued to make progress but still had a way to go before he was completely out of danger. Dr. Reynolds remained on the case in his own fashion—staying involved but as out of the way as possible.

And she wrote beautifully and warmly about what I had done in helping her but mostly for not printing a word in the *Tribune,* or anywhere else, about her dad. She thanked me for honoring both the spirit and the letter of our off-the-record agreement. "You are a most honorable and good man, Jack, and I regret very much having thought otherwise," she wrote.

I answered with a brief note of thanks with an apology for

not having told her directly that I was definitely not going to go with her dad's story. I told her I had gone back into the marines but offered no explanation. There was no mention of Vietnam but I assumed she probably figured that out.

There was no further response required or expected from her, and we each continued on with our very separate lives.

9

I thought often about Marti over the years but it was not until late 2008, forty years later, that she came back into my life.

It's a difficult story to tell—but, as they say in federal budget deficit politics, if not now, when?

I served two tours in Vietnam, my second as a battalion commander, the high point of what turned out to be a twenty-two-year career as an active-duty marine infantry officer. I retired in 1990 as a brigadier general assigned mostly to writing special speeches and other high-level PR kinds of things for the commandant of the Marine Corps in Washington.

Jan, my wife, and I chose Charlottesville as our retirement home, a most glorious place to live. The magnificent green landscapes and cool breezes of southwest Virginia combined with the intellectual stimulation provided by the University of Virginia's faculty, libraries, and events—debates, lectures, performances—was perfect for us.

From Charlottesville, only a two-hour drive from Washington, I developed a substantial second working life as a freelance writer and former-general television commentator. My TV appearances on military issues, mostly on cable, Sunday-morning network shows, and PBS, have especially helped augment my marine retirement pay. I was used by the media extensively during the Iraq war as a critic of George W. Bush's sending Americans into harm's way based on unproven intelligence. Later, my public support of allowing gays and lesbians to serve openly in the military drew many invitations. Those kinds of positions were not expected from a retired marine one-star with much combat experience.

The Jerry Compton dream to write a novel pretty much disappeared when I left the news business. The closest I came was outlining a fictional story of a Kansas bank president who posed as a former marine combat officer in order to increase his business and local civic prestige. He not only learned the marine lingo and culture but also bought a small metal Silver Star lapel pin on eBay that he wore on his suit coats. It all ended badly for him, as it should have, but he was a good phony marine and it took a while for him to get found out. I thought of it as a novel of expectations but I never got around to sending the outline to an agent or a publisher.

While going through some of my old papers for a possible nonfiction Vietnam memoir, I came across my unused reporting notes from the bubble top adventure. I duly remembered what Bernie Shapiro, the *Tribune* bureau chief, had said about my holding the story for a book. I laughed at how long that meant I had been holding it now. Too long, too late? Maybe not.

And I wondered, for possibly the millionth time, about what had happened to Marti Van Walters.

A skilled user of the Internet (one of my grandsons calls me General Google), I easily located Marti Van (Walters) Jackson, a professor of English at the University of Pennsylvania in Philadelphia. Her official bio on the Penn website said she had earned her master's at Penn, gotten a PhD at the University of Chicago, and then returned to Penn as a member of the faculty. She had remained there ever since with her husband, a physics professor named Lou Jackson. The Penn bio said Marti had written extensively about modern American women writers, most particularly Katherine Anne Porter and Eudora Welty. The Jacksons had two daughters as did, interestingly enough, Jan and I.

My phone call to Marti—done cold with no email warning—got a surprised but most bubbly, joyous, great-to-hear-from-you response. She said something about having seen me on television and that she "more often than not, agreed with you." We decided to meet for lunch in Philadelphia sometime "just to catch up," but I pushed it further. I said—lied— that I had to come to Philadelphia in a few weeks to do some research about a piece I was writing on Tun Tavern, the place where, legend has it, the first U.S. Marines—mostly while drunk—were recruited in 1775. She agreed.

"I'd have known you anywhere," she said to me three weeks later when we greeted each other at the upscale French brasserie on Rittenhouse Square she had suggested.

"Same with you," I said, returning the favor. "I'd have rec-ognized you from ten miles away."

Actually, it wasn't just a favor. She really did look remark-ably the same as she had forty years before. Her hair was gray-ing but still short, and her face, while showing a few wrinkles, still blossomed like a happy flower. Her sixty-year-old body, which I silently admired through a light green pantsuit, could have passed for a twenty-year-old's.

The marine "exercise thing," as my family called it, had kept me in pretty good shape, too, if I do say so myself. My hair, also short, was mostly white but it was still there, as were the flat stomach and good build. And I hadn't lost even a frac-tion of an inch off my six-foot height.

I had, without much thought, put on a tweed sport coat with charcoal slacks and an open-collar sport shirt. I didn't realize until I was on the train that my outfit was only a slight change from my old reporter's Glory Suit.

"If I am sixty, and I am, then that makes you seventy," Marti said with a laugh.

"And I am," I said, picking up the joke.

"Remember how we talked about the ten-year age differ-ence?" Marti asked.

I assured her that I definitely remembered.

"Was that the real reason you kept deflecting me when I threw myself at you and your bed?" she asked. "I'm sorry, but I just have to know."

"Trust me, Marti, there is nothing I would have loved more

than taking you up on . . . well, you. But I kept thinking you were just a college kid and it would have been taking unfair advantage or something like that." I left out the part about the ethical qualms of a journalist sleeping with a source—which, to me, she still was at the time.

"Have you done many what-ifs about me?" she asked.

I wasn't ready for that one. While much had gone under many bridges in the last forty years, the question brought me up short. Perhaps not all of the water was gone?

"No, not really," I dodged. "My mind was kept too busy with being a marine."

Then, to swat her question away even further, I asked, "Notice anything new about me?"

She gave me a hard look and said, "Frankly, no. You look great—the same . . ."

I looked down at my wristwatch and said, "It's over twenty minutes and I have yet to excuse myself for a smoking break."

"You quit?"

"Yes, ma'am."

"When?"

"Seventeen years, seven months, and four days ago."

She extended her right hand, which I took in mine. "Congratulations, Jack," she said with that great smile. But I knew she was probably thinking that I'd quit way too late to completely rule out lung cancer turning up down the road. At least she didn't say it.

Marti went on to give me a full bubble top family update, which made me very happy. She said it had taken more than five years, but Martin Van Walters had come back almost completely to life. For several years before retiring, he worked successfully as a consultant to corporations on personal security for CEOs and other executives. He died peacefully in his sleep of a heart attack three years before at age seventy-nine. He was buried in that same Kinderhook cemetery with Martin "O.K." Van Buren. Rosemary Walters, she said, had been completely alcohol-free since Reynolds got her involved in Alcoholics Anonymous. As a widow, she still attended AA meetings regularly at her retirement village condo in Delaware, a short train ride from Marti in Philadelphia.

"I always felt your mother got lost in the shuffle of everything that was happening to your dad," I said. "I wasn't sure anybody was paying much attention to her and her problems."

"You were absolutely right," Marti said. "Reynolds said victims usually come in pairs. Nobody gets sick like Dad did all by himself."

Marti and I talked about some other things, including the dwindling state of play on Kennedy assassination conspiracy theories.

"There's been no deathbed confession from an Oswald helper yet, as far as I know," I said.

"There's still time before we hit the full fifty-year mark," Marti said. "There could still be one out there."

I told her I didn't think so. Whatever the various conspiracy theorists continued to put out, there was no credible evidence to refute the theory that Oswald acted alone. Yes, one man really did fire three rifle shots out a Dallas window in a few seconds and change the course of history—forever. For me, the fragility of what we all come to think of as order and normality has been the permanent lesson of the Kennedy assassination. Since that awful day we've known we are always only three shots away from chaos.

Marti also brought up the Iraq war, which was in full military and political momentum. I told her what I had been saying about it on television and in op-ed newspaper pieces, but she seemed already aware of my "reasoned antiwar" position, as she called it. Her get-the-troops-out-of-there views were much stronger than mine.

"Can I assume you were for McCain—with the military connection?" she asked, smiling her Marti smile. "I was out canvassing for Obama most weekends all over Pennsylvania."

I grinned but said not a word, having decided as a matter of my own personal policy to let all of that lie. I, too, was for Obama, but not publicly. From having been a reporter and then a career military officer, I had a natural resistance to declaring political preferences. My punditing also led me to keep the lid on my politics. Being labeled a Republican or Democratic general was not good for my business. I wanted to be seen as a nonpartisan evenhanded basher/defender of war decisions and the people who make and execute them.

"When you were a marine in Vietnam, did you think about dying?" Boom. All of a sudden, there she was again, the straightforward, in-your-face girl from forty years ago. Yes, Marti was still very much Marti.

"No, not at all," I said, ready to quickly end this line of

conversation. Marines are taught from their first recruit depot formation that there's nothing more useless than a dead marine or one who constantly thinks and talks about being one.

"So you enjoyed it? Being a marine?" she asked.

What was I supposed to say? "Sure, except being transferred from one post or country to another all the time." And then, without really thinking, "That kind of life would not have fit in with that of a college English professor."

"Ah! So you *did* do some what-if thinking about me!" She said it with a pleasure that gave me pleasure.

"You got me," I said with a grin. "Now, how about you?"

She looked right at me and said: "My only what-if regret is that I did not end up going to bed with you at Kinderhook." I felt some warmth spread to my face—and elsewhere.

Marti went on.

"Despite all my talk about the openness of the sixties, I was still very slowly finding my way from virginity," she continued with a huge smile. She was clearly loving this. "I figured I could justify doing it with you because I owed you so much. And because you were so much older—and a marine— you could teach me more about what I needed to know about sex."

"Semper Fi," I said with a laugh. A real one.

"What if we had slept together at Kinderhook?"

"What if we did?" I asked.

"Would it have led to anything more?"

"Who knows?"

"What if it did and, because of that, you didn't go back in

the marines?" Marti persisted, her face still in full impish mode.

That did it. She had hit the nerve that mattered the most to me. "I'd have figured out a way to be with you in Philadelphia, probably as the executive editor—or, better still, an outspoken left-wing columnist—with *The Philadelphia Inquirer,*" I said. It was a phony hold-the-line answer.

"You'd have done that just for me?"

"What if you had decided to give up the idea of advanced degrees and become a military wife? How would you have been as a white-gloves hostess at receptions on marine bases?"

"What if you had been killed in Vietnam?"

There we were again. I ducked. "What if you jumped in bed with an American literature professor while I was overseas fighting for my country?"

"I would never have done that to you!" she said with some force. And I believed her. It probably didn't make sense, but I did.

Then she moved on to where my mind had spent countless hours over the last forty years.

"What if you'd ignored off-the-record and published my dad's story in the paper then—in 1968?" Marti asked.

Finally, here we were.

"You would have hated me for the rest of our lives," I declared.

"True. Oh, how true that is. You might have died from a Finnish sniper rifle shot by me on a street corner in Washington—instead of from the Vietcong or whoever in Vietnam."

"I didn't die in Vietnam, please remember."

"But you might have . . ."

Marti abruptly looked away from me. She was thinking of something—something new and important. I had not seen her in forty years, but I knew that look. I had seen it at Union Station, in Philadelphia, and, of course, in Kinderhook.

She came right at me. "Why did you suddenly decide to go back into the marines? You never mentioned even thinking about the marines again to me."

I shrugged.

"I thought for sure that you were going to break our off-the-record agreement and do our story," she pressed.

Now it was my turn to look away.

I was having a great time with Marti. That was all I was trying to think about. She was as charming and quick-witted as I had remembered her.

"Did you win the Medal of Honor?" she asked me, finally, when she realized I wasn't going to explain myself to her.

"No, no," I said, and then my ego and pride could not resist adding, "But I did pick up a Silver Star, one or two Bronze Stars, and a couple of Purple Hearts."

"So you were wounded?"

"A few times. But I didn't die, as you've noticed. The hits were nothing serious. Everything healed."

And, before I knew it, our lunch together passed the two-hour mark.

I realized that, with all our happy and serious talk, neither of us asked for or volunteered any information about our respective immediate families.

She didn't ask me about Jan, my wife of thirty-five years, and how we met on a blind date at a Marine Corps birthday ball in San Diego, or about our children or grandchildren. Her husband, the physics professor, and their two children never came up, either. I realized that I had absolutely no desire to know a single thing about that part of her life.

The fact is that for two hours neither of us strayed much from our original roles from forty years before. We remained at Kinderhook, mostly in that cold tiny room on the third floor.

And damned if I couldn't feel that Marti, always and ever the smart kid, could sense something still to come. Of course, she would be wondering why else I would suddenly call her after all these years . . .

"I take it you've got something on your mind, Jack, besides renewing an old acquaintance and playing a game of what-if with me." By God, she was reading my mind! "I'll bet money it's about writing a book—am I right?"

I shook my head in wonder—in admiration, in affection.

"You want to tell our story, don't you? You want me to finally release you from the off-the-record deal?"

She had it—of course. With her, it had always been of course.

"You got it," I said. "That would be great."

She reached down for a black canvas briefcase she had brought with her, something I had barely noticed when she arrived. She set it on her lap, unzipped it, and pulled out a sheaf of papers that looked to be at least two inches thick. There were also at least half a dozen bound diaries.

"Be my guest, Jack. I took notes about everything that happened to me, particularly beginning November twenty-second, 1963, including after Dad came back to Kinderhook from Singapore. Use them in any way you wish. All I ask is that you return them when you're finished. Keep them in the case—easier to carry."

"If you weren't so much younger than me I'd grab you and hug you," I joked.

"You had your chance and passed on that, Jack." She laughed.

I thanked her for the material and the cooperation seven or eight times in different ways, including putting a hand on hers across the table. It was a gesture of gratitude and I assumed she took it that way. We were not about to jump in bed for a nooner—no matter old memories from a cold room, right?

"Got a title for the book?" she asked, getting ready to leave.

"No, no. I've got to put it all together and write the damn thing first. Then find a publisher, which might not be that easy. Our big bubble top story might not seem as fascinating now as it would have forty years ago."

Marti said: "How about *The Great Lindenwald Shooting* for a title?"

"That could work, we'll see," I said, writing it down on a notebook that I pulled out of a pocket. A carryover from my reporting days. Old habits die hard.

"*Shootout at the O.K. Mansion?*"

I laughed—but didn't write it down.

"*Top Down?*" she said. "That's *it*!"

I said, "Okay, but it might sound to some people like something to do with a women's brassiere."

"General, you have a young marine's mind, you dirty old marine," Marti said.

We both laughed, stood, and said good-bye with a good hug.

And then she sat right back down. "Jack, there's something here that doesn't quite add up."

I sat down, too.

"You're right about doing a book now about us—Dad and all the rest. That story may, in fact, already be gone forever. So?"

"So? What do you mean, 'so'?"

"So . . . well, I don't know." It was clear to me that she was thinking about something else.

She sighed and was back on her feet. Whatever else was in her mind had not yet come into full focus.

"It was great to see you again," Marti said.

"Same here." And I meant that so very much. This had been a treat for me in every way.

We parted for a second time in forty years but with no second big hug.

But before I could get the check from the waiter she was back. She was crying huge tears. She raised her hands and arms toward me and embraced me with a force of affection that nearly knocked me over.

"I just figured it out, Jack," she said looking up at me, her voice quiet and soft. "You ran away to the marines to avoid running our story in the paper. If you had stayed a reporter you would have done it, you would have had to do it. You would have wiggled out of that off-the-record stuff. You risked your life in Vietnam to keep yourself from doing something really, really awful that would have made you feel guilty and would have made me hate you for life."

And then she was really gone. This time for good.

Smart Marti was right—almost. I also had figured that if I was going to war anyway, I might as well do it the old-fashioned way—with the marines. But now that Marti had laid out what had really happened so directly and out loud, I could no longer fool myself. Yes, I ran away. And I had been swatting away at it for the last forty years.

I signed the restaurant check, which was pretty hefty. Each of us had had two courses and two glasses of a good Chardonnay. Marti had an espresso and I had coffee afterward.

And I thought: *Who knows where I might be right now if I had decided as a journalist to live with my guilt and Marti's hate and, in 1968, told the full story of former Secret Service agent Martin Van Walters?* And what if later I had written a few novels, hanging in there on the Hemingway model? Would I really have ended up in Paris? With whom? Who knows, who knows? What if, what if?

I picked up Marti's briefcase and walked out onto the sidewalk into the Philadelphia sunshine. It was a great day, perfect for walking.

Author's Note

Top Down is fiction, but there are some autobiographical elements that deserve mention.

I was, in fact, working as a reporter on the afternoon newspaper in Dallas (*The Dallas Times Herald,* now no more) on November 22, 1963. My assignment was Love Field, and I did have a bubble top experience with a Secret Service agent similar to the one I described. That was the rough seed for this novel, but the details, as well as Martin Van Walters, his family, and their story, were completely made up. So were almost all of the Secret Service agents and other characters. The only real people were mostly Warren Commission officials and those involved in the investigation.

Also, for the record, I did serve for three years as an infantry officer in the Marine Corps during that time of peace between the Korean and Vietnam wars. But unlike my fictional character Jack Gilmore, I did not return to active duty and go to Vietnam, win medals, or become a general.

There are several people who were generous in their assistance to me. I hereby thank them but with the full caveat that

189

none deserves blame for any of the fictional paths or liberties I took. That is particularly true of the gentleman psychiatrist and PTSD expert Dr. Frank Ochberg and his associate Joyce Boaz. Other blameless helpers were: the staff of the Sixth Floor Museum in Dallas including Gary Mack, Nicola Langford, and Christina Carneal; Park Ranger Dawn Sackawitch, Dan Dattilio, and the other terrific National Park Service folks at Lindenwald; the Speer family, active members of the Kinderhook Reformed Church who happened to be there when I wandered in; my writer grandson Luke O'Brien, who was a co-observer on one of my Kinderhook visits; and historian Michael Beschloss, my great friend and thoughtful adviser, most particularly on matters concerning the Kennedy assassination.

My reading involved a variety of books, reports, articles, and videos about the assassination, mental health issues, and the Secret Service. I am particularly grateful for the personal accounts of former agent Clint Hill.

I also owe a tremendous debt and thanks to the steady, creative work of Kendra Harpster, my editor at Random House.

JIM LEHRER, 2013

ABOUT THE AUTHOR

Top Down is JIM LEHRER's twenty-first novel. He is also the author of three nonfiction books and four plays. He began his work in journalism as a newspaper reporter in Texas. He then worked for more than forty years in public television and is currently the executive editor of *PBS NewsHour*. He lives in Washington, D.C., with his novelist wife, Kate. They have three daughters.

About the Type

This book was set in Sabon, a typeface designed by the well-known German typographer Jan Tschichold (1902–74). Sabon's design is based upon the original letter forms of Claude Garamond and was created specifically to be used for three sources: foundry type for hand composition, Linotype, and Monotype. Tschichold named his typeface for the famous Frankfurt typefounder Jacques Sabon, who died in 1580.